Two a Penny

Two a Penny

by

Stella Linden
and David Winter

HODDER AND STOUGHTON
LONDON SYDNEY AUCKLAND TORONTO

The traffic roared by on both sides, taxis, lorries and buses—
you could just see their top decks over the stark walls.

£100,000 for twopence.

FLY BEA TO SUNNY CYPRUS

London's New Smash-hit Musical.

THE MOUSETRAP—17th GREAT YEAR

It was all happening out there, on the sides of the buses
and in the faces of the West End lunch crowds. There was
noise and diesel fumes and colour this suddenly warm London June day. The man outside Littlewoods with his armful
of cheap nylons, eyes like radar scanners for police helmets
in the crowd, had put it rather well.

"Summer's 'ere, girls. Make the most of it. Show 'em a
bit more leg. Come on, 'alf a dollar a pair."

But it's not happening in here, thought Carol Turner,
looking up at the crumbling walls, the grey spire sharp
against an unbelievably blue sky, and down at the dank
undergrowth and the broken old flagstones with their
dreary memorials. Despite the warmth she shivered, and
wriggled her shoulders a little deeper into her cardigan.

Sometimes she wondered why Jamie was so keen on the
place. Of course, he was very proud of the fact that he'd
found it. She remembered the moment and couldn't resist a
grin.

They'd been walking down Shaftesbury Avenue and
Jamie had been going on about some fabulous new opening
he was working in stock car racing. He'd met this fellow
at the Fashion College who was going to set him up in a big
way. She couldn't recollect the details, but she was pretty
sure it came just before the travel agency breakthrough and
a few days after the chain of betting shops fell through because of the incompetence of his associates.

At any rate, they'd been walking along talking . . . well, Jamie talking and she was listening and watching the shop windows, when suddenly Jamie disappeared. Cut off in mid-sentence. She had looked around and just spotted him weaving his way through a group of people and into an alley.

She had decided to give chase. After all, the last time Jamie had done anything like that she hadn't seen him for a fortnight. With rather more courtesy but a good deal less speed she had struggled into the alley, too . . . but Jamie had gone. There was a man cleaning a window, and a young couple gazing into each other's eyes in a doorway, but nobody else in sight.

Carol had walked a few yards up the alley and was just deciding to cut her losses and go into the Wimpy bar for a coke when she heard a hoarse whisper almost at her shoulder.

"Carol . . . Carol."

She stopped.

"Carol, I'm in here. Quick."

A sheet of corrugated iron blocking a hole in a stone wall appeared to vibrate and then bent back to leave a thirty inch gap. Putting both hands to it, she managed to widen the breach and squeezed inside.

"Jamie," she had warned, "if this is some crazy stunt . . ."

For an answer he had laid a finger on her lips for silence.

"Ssh, little bird. Danger lurks out yonder."

"Danger?"

"I saw him coming. Mick."

"Mick *who*?"

"I dunno, do I. He's a porter at the College." Jamie dropped his voice. "Owe him a couple of quid, you know. He's a bit touchy about it."

She had walked a few paces into the yard, though it wasn't a yard.

"How long? How long has he been waiting for it then?"

Jamie followed her. "You know, I've stumbled on something here, haven't I? I mean, just cop a load of this lot. Nobody's been here since the War."

6

"How long?" she had repeated.

"Twenty years ago, wasn't it?"

Carol hadn't smiled.

"How long have you owed it to him?"

Jamie had shrugged. "A few weeks . . . well, say a couple of months at the most . . . He'll get it back. I'm not dishonest, you know. It's just that, well, I was going to ask you anyway."

"It's no good, I'm short this week. Cynthia's leaving to have a baby and we had a whip round. That's the third in a month in our department."

"Just mind you're not the fourth, little bird," he had said, and then changed the subject again.

They'd explored the 'yard', there and then. It was a bombed church, they supposed, absolutely untouched, just the way Hitler had left it. There was no roof at all, but there were four walls, and two of them were quite high, with great stone window frames trapping sudden scenes of clouds, or office roofs, or top decks of buses, according to the angles and where you happened to be standing. Jamie had there and then named it *their* place. After all, he had argued, probably nobody knew about it. The records had got destroyed in the blitz. There had been a blunder by some stupid civil servant. And now it stood there, like a pre-fabricated film set, waiting to be exploited by a creative genius.

Not only that, but it was a nice quiet place to eat your sandwiches and "muck about a bit" in the lunch break.

Yes, Carol thought, Jamie liked the place, but liking it still didn't make him turn up on time. She looked at her watch. Ten past one. She was due back at half past, and with the Summer sale on she daren't be late.

Carol was sitting on a fallen boulder near where the main aisle had once been. She found the place a bit creepy, really, especially when Jamie was "mucking about." It didn't seem right somehow, not in a church. Not even a dead one.

And it was dead. That was the odd thing about it. It was all happening outside, this suddenly Summer day, but inside it was dead.

She looked again at the memorial stone under her feet.

Sacred to the memory of
SAMUEL SEBASTIAN GREY
Churchwarden of this parish
and Freeman of the City of West-
minster. Born 1702. Died 1767.
"Their works do follow them"

Again she shivered. That last sentence seemed to have a sinister sound, like a veiled threat. She tried to imagine Samuel Sebastian Grey, who died exactly two hundred years ago and bits of whom lay beneath her feet. This had been his church, she supposed. Now, look at it. The floor overgrown, the air thick with rotting greenery and cats and midSummer pollen, the flag-stones broken and all the man-made order deformed. "Their works do follow them."

It was all happening outside, this suddenly Summer day, but the church had no part in it. It was like a barren, lifeless island in a flowing sea of life. It was another world, another age, another kind of dying.

"Carol."

She started and turned her head, eyes coming alive and body suddenly alert and responsive.

"Jamie! I thought you weren't coming."

"Who, me?" Suddenly the oldest game was being played, eyes, hands just touching, words, calculated yet seemingly casual, and things that say more than anyone intended. "Me, not turn up. What makes you think I'd do a thing like that?"

Carol laughed, knowing but not saying, not wanting to play the game wrongly.

"Have a sandwich. Cheese and tomato."

Jamie peered into the bag, but shook his head.

"Can't stop, little bird. I've got a business call to make. I really just stopped by to see if you can lend me a couple of quid."

"You haven't paid me back yet from last time," she said, but she opened her purse and looked inside. Jamie looked, too.

"Here, you've got two more to spare. It's Friday tomorrow. I'll let you have it back by Monday."

"Jamie." The name was half a protest, half a rebuke. But the way she looked at him as she said it—eye-brows crumpled, eyes full of simple adoration—turned it into an expression of abject surrender. At any rate, Carol offered no further resistance as he slid the two notes from her purse, folded them and stuffed them into the breast pocket of his corduroy suit.

He lent forward slightly and kissed her on the forehead.

"Well, t'rar little bird. Must be off."

As he disappeared past a clump of bushes, Carol called after him, "Shall I see you tonight then?"

He just paused, almost out of view, to wave his fingers at her and jerk his head in a gesture that could have meant anything. And then he was gone.

Carol began to gather up her lunch things. Another perfectly good packet of sandwiches wasted, another perfectly good lunch hour ruined. She threw a whole sandwich to a group of sparrows who were scratching around near an empty zinc tank, and watched them converge on it, tearing at it and fighting for the largest pieces. As she waited two or three pigeons also arrived, and the smaller birds, grateful perhaps for the morsels they already had, flew away to watch the bigger birds finish off the meal. For a moment she thought of throwing a stone to chase off the interlopers. She felt sorry for the sparrows. But why should she, she corrected herself, when it would change nothing? The sparrows would still be tiny and helpless. The pigeons would just return another day and steal a different treat. The little ones must learn to be little and happy, and the big ones must accept their existence.

She glanced at her watch. Five minutes. She should just make it. She looked again at the sandwiches that were left, and on an impulse tore open the bag and hurled the contents into the bushes. Startled, the birds—both sizes—took to the wing and hovered uncertainly.

"Go on," she told them, "It's good food. Make the most of it."

As she pushed her way along Oxford Street Carol's spirits

9

rose. After all, why should she feel it was a ruined lunch hour? Jamie had turned up. He hadn't said he wouldn't see her tonight. He had been as friendly as usual.

And he had got two quid for it.

Spirits sank again. Cheap at the price, wasn't it? He gave her three or four minutes of his precious time, a bit of chat, a peck on the forehead and the vague hope of part of an evening together. She gave him two quid. Suddenly she felt like a call girl.

It was no good fooling herself. She was a hopeless case. No matter how bitter and angry she felt about the way he treated her, when he was there it all disappeared. The girls at work warned her about him, but she took no notice. She knew lots of them would gladly swap with her. When he was around, everything was in colour, it was all happening— even if it *was* only day-dreams. For that she could overlook all the sham.

He was a sham, of course. She knew that, really. The flashy clothes—paid for with her money, non-existent credit and his mother's pay from her receptionist's job; the mod patter, picked up second-hand in Denmark Street and at the fashion college; and the brilliant plans for the future which always foundered on the borders of the promised land: there was no substance to it all, Carol knew that.

But with Jamie she was always able to believe it could happen, and that was all she asked for. He was alive, and involved in life, in a way no-one in her life before had ever been, except perhaps Aunt Sarah. And when you're nineteen and your parents are dead, and you work in a dreary hole like Barry and Swallows, it's hope you really want, and *life*. Jamie—handsome, in his dark sort of way, cheeky, restless, elusive—was worth a hundred ruined lunch hours and mountains of wasted sandwiches.

So, having gone through three moods in just double that number of minutes, and completed a trick she was getting rather proud of lately (proving to herself that loving Jamie was the best and most worthwhile thing she had ever done, in the face of all the evidence), Carol Turner ducked into the staff entrance of Barry and Swallows, the time on the doorman's Everite watch showing her to be two minutes and thirty three seconds late for the afternoon shift.

At exactly the same moment Jamie was walking along Piccadilly, except that Jamie never walked. Camera silently smooth beside him, he was passing through a crowd of extras, a daring smile playing on his lips as he thought of the rendezvous that lay ahead. A passing girl, prettier than average, caught his attention and he grinned impertinently. She blushed and smiled, and he side-stepped a man reading a paper and lost her in the crowd. Then, with dramatic and quite superfluous suddenness, he swung on his heel and made his way down an alley into Jermyn Street.

As he crossed the road the scene ended. The street, the extras and the pretty girls were one world. But Fitch and his hat shop were another matter altogether. The camera and the royal premiere of his first film would have to wait. Just now he wanted money, and Fitch seemed the best way to get it in satisfactory quantities.

He paused on the doorstep to check on his reflection in the dark window of the shop, then pushed the door, which sent the old world bell jingling, and went in.

Fitch's hat shop was select. That is to say, the hats were priced to deter all but the favoured few. It was quiet and obtrusively pre-War, the predominant colour being oak brown and the predominant smell, Turkish tobacco.

Hubert, Fitch's elegant assistant, raised an eyebrow as Jamie entered and, without a word, disappeared into the back of the shop. Jamie imitated the lift of an eye-brow into the gold-framed mirror behind the counter and awaited the appearance of Fitch himself.

"I didn't expect you, Hopkins." Jamie turned round with all the casual aplomb he could muster to face the man himself. "What is it this time? Money?"

The smoothly silent cameras were whirring again as Jamie paused and let a sardonic smile play on his lips.

"Understanding, that's what I like about you, Mr Fitch."

"I'm not a charitable institution," Fitch said, selecting a black Turkish cigarette from the box on the counter and beginning the ritual of lighting it.

"I'm prepared to earn it."

"A praise-worthy attitude, Hopkins."

Jamie took a step nearer, and leant towards Fitch confidentially.

"We've done a bit of business here and there, haven't we? Nothing much, I admit, but enough for you to know you can trust me." He dropped his voice even further. "I was wondering if you had something a bit more interesting?"

Fitch stared blandly at him.

"And what would you consider more interesting?"

"Let me make a run for you—a little delivery now and then."

"You live with your mother, Hopkins. Now there's a possible source of trouble."

Jamie resisted the urge to ask how Fitch knew about his mother and instead went on the defensive.

"My mum gets on with her life, and lets me get on with mine. Besides, she thinks I spend all my time at the Fashion College. She can't wait for the day I open my string of classy boutiques."

"And how about you, Hopkins. Can you wait for the day?"

"Well, there's today and there's tomorrow," replied Jamie darkly. "I mean, they're different, aren't they? Tomorrow I might want to get on with fashion, or I might not. How can I possibly know what I'll want tomorrow, if you see what I mean."

"Do you know what you want today?"

"Everyone knows that," said Jamie, and then, going for the big prize, "even your junkie friends."

Fitch drew on his elegant cigarette (for all the world like a character in a 'B' movie, Jamie thought) and studied him intently.

"You don't use anything yourself, do you?"

Jamie didn't answer the question, beyond a shake of the head.

"You'll give me a chance then, Mr Fitch."

Fitch looked at him coldly.

"Shall we say we'll see how we get along? Hubert will explain things to you."

At the sound of his name Hubert emerged from the room at the back and with a jerk of the head invited Jamie to join him. Hardly able to contain his excitement, feet on the verge of that promised land again, Jamie winked at Fitch and the silently whirring cameras followed him across the room.

The packet in his pocket pressed into his thigh, all the world watching, and the cameras. Through the hot crowds of this Soho afternoon, head down a little and eyes alert, Jamie felt the importance of the occasion. True, it was just a beginning. But already his mind was racing ahead, making plans. He had no intention of staying in the runner class, doing Fitch's dirty work and taking all the risks. But he had to start somewhere, and Fitch knew everybody who mattered in this game.

Outside the betting shop he paused and glanced around, checking he was not being followed, giving the camera his profile for a second, and then darted inside.

It was a miserable little place really, with its tired joke cards, picture of Kestrel and sundry stern notices on the walls, the air stale, the light dim and the floor littered with discarded midday papers and betting slips. Jamie took it in at a glance and also noted that the only pleasing feature was the bored blonde behind the grille at the counter. He decided to mix business with pleasure, in the Bond tradition.

"Hello," he said. She raised her head, eyes bored, hair lacquer cracking.

Jamie grinned. "I'm not going to pretend we met before."

She didn't smile, but appraised him slowly and impersonally.

"That's refreshing."

"I'm not in the habit of talking to strange women, so I haven't got anything prepared."

Reluctantly, she joined in the game "Pity."

Jamie stood on tiptoe and craned his neck to look over the counter.

"Five bob says your skirt's five inches above the knee."

At last, the response he had been playing for, the girl eyeing him, the face nearly interested.

"Cheeky!" she said, and then her face went plastic again. Jamie looked around to see the cause, and found it.

13

"Oh, Mr Jenkins," he said. "It's you I've come to see."

Jenkins looked at him suspiciously. "Do I know you?"

"Fitch sent me."

"All right, all right," Jenkins said, in a much lower tone, guiding Jamie away from the counter by the elbow and towards a side door, "No need to shout it about the place. And next time," he added, as they entered his tiny, smoke-filled office, "don't get so matey with the staff."

Jamie pulled the packet from his pocket and was surprised to find a wad of notes in his hand almost before he realised the transaction had begun. Afraid that the whole thing might be over before he had played his full hand, Jamie started to count the notes, while Jenkins watched impatiently.

"I've wanted to meet you for some time, Mr Jenkins, a matter of business. I feel you're a man to be trusted—with something personal, I mean."

He paused, waiting for a response from Jenkins, but got none.

Jamie waved the wad of notes. "I've got the chance to turn this over, just in the next few hours."

For a moment Jenkins was interested. "Fitch's money? You've got to be joking."

Now Jamie was beginning to enjoy the part being thrust upon him.

"Thinking about it quite calmly, Mr Jenkins, it's not really Fitch's until I hand it over, is it? And where's the risk? I've got the customer, the money. You get me a connection, and we'll both realise a few pounds with Fitch none the wiser."

Jenkins, however, had become impassive again.

"I'll think about it."

"Time's important," Jamie countered. "I wouldn't dream of asking Fitch to go to bed tonight without his loot. Suppose I ring you. About seven?"

Jenkins opened the door, the interview over.

"Up to you," he said.

2

"Is that you, Jamie?" His mother's voice from the kitchen came spot on cue, as usual. He stuck his tongue out in the general direction of the sound but replied with endearing sweetness.

"Sorry I'm late, Mum."

He remembered the wad of notes in his pocket, pulled them out, thought a moment and then folded them and stuffed them into his shoe. You couldn't be too careful, especially with mothers.

"Where've you been? It's half past six."

"Swotting in that stupid library at the college," he replied, strolling into the kitchen confidently and kissing her on the cheek.

Jamie threw his jacket on to a chair and began to wash his hands at the kitchen sink, observing his mother's reactions carefully in the mirror.

"They really ought to do something about that place, you know," he said. "You could grow spuds on the shelves. Here, Mum . . ."—a change of key, softer, wheedling, full of sincerity—"can you spare a couple of quid?"

Ruby, who was sitting at the table repairing her nail lacquer, looked up sharply. The scene had been performed plenty of times, but it still required careful playing.

"What for?"

Jamie kept a wary eye on the mirror. "Books. I can't keep up my studies without the books, can I?"

He dried his hands slowly, not wanting to turn to face her, his eyes following every trace of feeling that her expression conveyed.

"Oh well," she said, sighing, but getting up, too, and going over to the bookcase above her bed in the communicating room. "I'm not made of money, you know."

Jamie watched in the mirror as she took a book down from the shelf and removed the notes from between its pages. Her secret hiding place was rather pathetic, he thought. He'd known about it since he was ten, but he had thought it better not to let her know. It might come in handy one day.

"There's a hot pie in the oven," said his mother as she came back with the money. Jamie took it gratefully, kissing her again and pushing the notes into his breast pocket.

"Thanks, Mum. Knew you'd understand. But I can't stop for supper—I'm late for a lecture already."

Again the sharp look, again the familiar scene to be played carefully.

"Lecture? That's a new one, isn't it?"

"Yeh. Greengrass. 'Techniques in Textiles'—load of codswallop, but it's on the syllabus. Just my luck."

Ruby sat down at the table again and watched him. She wanted to believe him. He was a good boy at heart. He'd always been thoughtful over little things, and what a comfort when Harry died. Nine—that's all Jamie was then—little dark head and endless chat and big, dark eyes. She didn't care what the neighbours said, he was a good boy really.

So her voice became softer and Jamie noticed again how she tried to cover up her native Peckham when she was setting out to make an impression—even on him.

"You do worry me, Jamie," she said. "Working hard like you do, studying. You ought to look after yourself better, you know."

Jamie looked at her, summed it all up and moved into the next scene—not so emotional, more comedy really, but still to be played with care.

"You can't talk," he said. "Up all hours of the day and night, gadding about with your admirers."

Ruby dropped her suburban mother role, her face brightening. "Get along with you," she said, enjoying it.

Jamie leant on the table.

"Business wouldn't be so good for that head shrinker of yours if he didn't have such a dishy receptionist. Shouldn't be surprised if he wasn't a bit sweet on you himself. You tell him to watch his step. I don't want any hanky panky behind the medicine cabinets."

"Jamie Hopkins," she protested, loving it, back in Peckham now. "Talking to your mother like that!"

Jamie moved towards the door, thinking about his exit line.

"Hey, he's not waiting outside ready to pounce the second my back's turned, is he?"

"I wish he was," said Ruby, meaning it but laughing.

"Tut, tut," Jamie countered, seeing his cue and making for the door, "the things you say, and me only an innocent lad!"

As the front door slammed behind him Ruby walked over to the mirror and patted her newly-permed hair complacently. Yes, he was a good boy really; thoughtful, and such a comfort.

Jamie was feeling good. What with the little bit of business with Fitch, his own plan for turning the takings over that very evening, the fact that he had got two quid he hadn't really expected (and, if he was honest, didn't really need) from his mum, and now Carol, he couldn't remember when he had felt better.

As he made his way into the Earls Court area, heading for Carol's digs, he turned his mind to the question of how he would play her tonight. Probably it was time for him to be nice to her again, the great lover, attentive to her every whim. It would certainly suit his mood . . . but not his plans, because it was hard to be attentive when your mind was on business, and at seven he was going to ring Jenkins and the next few hours might be busy ones.

So he might play it cool. Not that Carol would mind. Sometimes she didn't even seem to notice, she was so glad just to be around. Embarrassing, sometimes—the way she'd look at him, in front of people, too.

Why didn't he chuck her, then? He'd often thought about that. She was no Miss World—all right, of course, but no raving beauty and even, from some angles, a bit plump. She wasn't even a great talker, but he had to admit she was a first-rate listener. She was what his mother would call a 'nice' girl—he'd tried hard enough, but she wasn't having any and he was pretty sure she never had with anybody.

So what was it? He arrived at the same conclusion as he always did at the end of this particular discussion with himself. Carol was there, and convenient, and presentable. He didn't have to go chasing her, wasting valuable time pursuing a reluctant victim. When your eyes are on the top that's an important thing. She was there when he wanted her, to listen to his ideas, reflect his achievements and provide an eager, attentive audience for his performances. After all, there was no point in having good schemes if nobody knew about them. And she looked all right—'thoroughly modern', like a little bird, bright and undemanding. It wouldn't do for a bloke in his position not to have a presentable bird. They might think he was queer, or something.

Just as he was turning into the mews where Carol lived he spotted a flower seller, and on an impulse bought a bunch of violets. A bit of fresh ammo never came amiss.

In the mews there were several cottages made out of old stables. James stood outside the first one and tossed a pebble on to the upstairs window. It opened and Carol appeared, her face a gratifying mixture of surprise and delight.

"Aren't you ready yet?" he asked.

"Ready? I didn't think you were coming."

"Not coming? You're always accusing me of not coming!"

Carol laughed, and the game was being played, the June sun reddening the roof tiles in its final moments, the mews hot and quiet. Jamie held up the violets.

"Look!"

"Lovely," Carol said. "Sha'n't be a tick. Don't go away."

She disappeared, and Jamie surveyed the violets cheerfully. The door opened, but it wasn't Carol.

"Hallo Mrs Burry."

"Oh, it's you." Carol's landlady surveyed him coolly. Jamie tried to imagine what she looked like under the cosmetics but gave up. He could imagine only too well what she looked like under her silk headscarf. She might have been born with those curlers in, he thought, you never see her without them.

"Yes, it's me," he said, "as if you hadn't been waiting for me at your turret window since dawn. Not disturbing you, am I?"

Mrs Burry permitted herself a sardonic smile.

"Long time since anyone disturbed me, dolly."

Jamie looked at her, and then at the violets in his hand. He couldn't resist the gesture, though it was a waste of a good half dollar. He bowed, and handed her the flowers.

"When I saw those violets, I said to myself, 'I bet Mrs Burry would really appreciate a nice bunch of them'."

Mrs Burry studied the flowers, wilting a little from Jamie's hand and the evening heat.

"Poor little devils, they look like I feel." She wasn't taken in by the gesture, but that didn't mean it was not appreciated. "Care to wait inside?"

Jamie followed her in. Mrs Burry's living room was new territory to him. It was like stepping back into history. Every wall bore mementoes of her professional career as a dancer, but none of them was less than twenty years old. It was as though history had stood still in 1944—a notion enhanced by Mrs Burry herself, who dressed and talked in the idiom of the war-time Naafi.

She went over to the sink in the corner, partly screened by a curtain, and put the violets in a vase. She carried it across the room like a triumphal offering.

"Well," she said, placing it solemnly on the sideboard, "I have had bigger bouquets in my time, though I can't say the floral tributes have exactly been pouring in since I left the business." She jerked a thumb towards a framed pin-up picture. "That's me, that was. Deirdre Burré, 'Pep, Punch and Personality'."

Jamie eyed it as a connoisseur.

"Not bad."

"Oh, I was doing all right until the War came."

"Really? Which war?" It was cheeky, but he liked taking risks.

"Do you mind? The last one . . . or so they say. I wonder. And I was just a slip of a kid at the time."

Jamie picked up a tin helmet, spinning it on a finger.

"Were you an air-raid warden, then?"

"Not me, dolly," she said, fielding the hat and replacing it on the bookcase, "I didn't like the costume. I was in ENSA —the entertainment branch . . . you know, cheering up the

19

boys. France, Cyprus, Tunisia. You name it, I've played it."
She rolled her eyes at him over the top of a tea towel. "Two
years in the desert and I never lost me yashmak."

The towel became a frilly skirt and, to Jamie's embarrassment, Mrs Burry burst into song.

"They're either too young or too old . . ."

She caught his expression and the melody petered out.

"Well," she said, defensively, "it may seem corny to you
now, but they were a great bunch of lads, I can tell you. We
could do with a few of their sort around now. They were
men, not long haired pansies, and if they hadn't done what
they did your lot wouldn't be walking about waving banners
today."

"Get off. From what I hear they had a ruddy marvellous
time. They'd all like to do it again. There's a teacher at
college who gives you his war record first time you meet him
and shows you his medal the second time. He stopped living
when they demobbed him."

"It's all very well to say that, but you haven't seen it happen. I have." She checked herself on the brink of eloquence,
and drew back with a nervous laugh. "Oh well, it's a great
life if you weaken just a little."

"Yeah"—relieved that it was all back to banter again—
"I bet you were the terror of the trenches."

"Trenches? We didn't . . . Look, you can go off people, you
know."

Jamie stood at the end of the table, half an insolent grin
on his face, giving her just enough attention to keep the
conversation going, watching her with amused neutrality, as
though trying to imagine what her world was like, a tourist
smiling as the strange ways of the foreigners are explained
to him. She's really quite old, he thought, past it; it's all
stopped happening for her.

But she was already back to when it was happening,
Waterloo Station in the black-out, with men and women in
uniform everywhere, urns of tea and hissing steam and
never enough time. And Jamie was a cheeky corporal in the
ack-ack, laughing and taking liberties and writing funny
letters from 'Somewhere in England', always talking about
what they would do after the war. After the war! There

wasn't any 'after', it all happened then, and her world was a world of cheeky young men and Naafi tea and 'Lily Marlene' and chits and inoculations and leave passes and a corporal taking liberties in the black-out.

"Well, I wouldn't know, would I?" Jamie said, breaking the spell. "I mean, I wasn't born till it was all over. A victory baby, me. Mum got me instead of a medal."

"I've got a medal," she countered, picking up the tempo again. "I'll show you it next time."

"You got a medal? What for?"

"Well it wasn't for good conduct, dolly. One night in the Naafi there was this sergeant, maddened with cocoa, and . . ."

Mrs Burry lost Jamie as Carol came down the stairs.

"Oh well," she said, "don't do anything I wouldn't do."

Jamie winked, and steered Carol towards the door.

"I won't, don't worry."

As the door slammed behind them Mrs Burry stared at her own portrait—'curvaceous' was the word.

"What worries me kills most people," she said.

"The Drum" was the pub where they usually went. Carol was not sure why, but it probably had something to do with the fact that Jamie was known there. She had noticed that he never liked having to compete with others for the limelight, and here he didn't have to. They knew him, they thought he was amusing and bright, and he went out of his way to please them. At "The Drum", and just about nowhere else, Jamie was somebody. She supposed that was why they went there a couple of times a week, and hardly ever to the pictures. Or perhaps it was cheaper.

Mind you, she didn't really mind, sat here with her half of shandy to last the evening, watching and listening as Jamie went through his repertoire.

First it was Mary, the barmaid.

"Hallo, love. Tell me, is it the Guinness that gives you that gorgeous complexion?"

"Cheeky. Hark at him."

"Well, it wouldn't be the lovely mountain air in here, would it?"

"Any complaints, then, Mr Hopkins?"

"No love, I like it dark and dirty."

Then it was the Regulars, two old dears who paid the price of a half-pint to sit near the bar the whole evening.

"Hi, girls. How's things?"

"About usual, Jamie. Gonna sing to us, are you?"

"On request, dears—if you twist my arm."

"What you got tonight? Can you do 'The White Cliffs of Dover'? Lovely song, that. Vera Lynn."

"Sorry, girls. Wrong generation. Wrong sex."

"Ooh, d'you here what he said?"

By then half the saloon would be watching and listening, and Jamie would hold court for a bit, showing off and loving it. Somebody would say, "Give us a song", and then he would force himself to belt out one of the top pops, backed by the perspiring trio who provided the 'music' part of the 'music and dancing' permitted in the licence over the door.

Carol enjoyed it, if only because it meant she could sit back and watch Jamie, and not have to worry whether she was pleasing or irritating him. That was one of her main problems, usually, and had been ever since they had first met.

"He's good, you know," Mary said to Carol, leaning over the bar confidentially. "He ought to take it up."

"Don't tell him. He's got about fifty careers going already."

"At fashion college, isn't he?" Mary asked.

"Well, that's where he starts from. It all depends what mood he's in."

"Never mind, he'll get to the top all right."

Carol grinned at her frankly. "Oh yeah? It's deciding which tree that bugs him."

Jamie pushed through the crowd building up around the bar.

"Talking about me, girls?"

"Who else?" Mary said. "Hope your ears were burning."

He leant over to Carol and half whispered, "I've just got to make a phone call. Business." Before she could ask him what business, or with whom, he was gone.

Within a minute he was back. Jenkins had been very abrupt, and had said something about "learning the hard way". He's the one who ought to learn, Jamie thought bitterly as he made his way back to the bar: learn that Fitch wasn't the only smart operator. But, still, it all sounded rather ominous.

"I've got to make this contact—now," he told Carol.

"Jamie, is something wrong?"

"Wrong? Whatever gave you that idea? I've had a bit of luck. On to something big. Just you wait here, have another drink, and I'll be back in half an hour."

"The last time you said that I didn't see you for a week," Carol said with some force, but noticed something in Jamie's eyes that changed her tone. "Jamie, something *is* wrong. I'm coming with you."

He grabbed her hand and almost dragged her off the stool.

"All right," he hissed. "Come if you want to, but don't blame me if you get"—he checked himself—"bored to death."

It was another lovely June evening, warm and yet with a breeze sufficient to cool the pavements under your feet and keep the clouds moving over your head. The western sky was red, and the shadows of big buildings were stretching further and further over the streets. On the main roads there were the usual summer crowds, the groups of immigrants sitting on the steps of old terraced houses talking and laughing, and old men filling their lungs with summer air, making the most of it because the cough comes back with the dark evenings and you can't afford to waste a hot June day when days of any sort are running out. And the music, odd distorted snatches of it, echoed across the walls from open windows and filled in the background.

That was the set, and the silently smooth cameras were rolling into place for Jamie as he steered Carol across it. This time, mind you, there were nerves—a dry mouth, a sick unease in his stomach. But at least this was the real thing. The tightness in his right shoe reminded him that the days of fantasy were over. He had wanted to get into the action, and now he was in, right up to his neck.

He rehearsed his speech to himself again.

"Well, Hubert, I've got the loot. No problems, really, once I'd made it clear to Jenkins that I was working for Mr Fitch, and nobody else. I think you'll find that's correct—I've deducted my usual percentage."

That much was all right. But supposing Hubert knew. Supposing what Jenkins was hinting at was that Fitch had been told of his scheme to make use of the money. Near panic swept across him. But why suppose anything? Jenkins wouldn't tell—it was not in his interests. And he had got the money with him, safe and sound.

"Jamie, something's wrong. I know it is."

He glared at Carol sullenly.

"Nothing's wrong. I told you. Now just wait here. I'm meeting somebody over the road, down that alley."

As he turned on his heel and dodged through the traffic Carol belatedly called to him. She wanted to ask questions, to offer help, but she knew he wouldn't welcome it, and she was out of her depth anyway.

She watched Jamie cross the far pavement and go into the alleyway, which was quite dark and very narrow. As he entered it, three men emerged from the shadows and followed him. Jamie turned and faced them. Carol stared, her vision broken by passing vehicles, speechless with anticipated horror.

She saw Jamie bend down to get something out of his shoe and then hand it to the tallest man. As he did, one of the others kicked him in the face, sending him sprawling on his back. The third picked him up by his lapels and lent him against the wall, and then suddenly—all sound drowned for Carol by the traffic, so that it was like watching a silent movie—he brought his knee up into the pit of Jamie's stomach.

Carol screamed, and the spell was broken. She dashed into the road to go to his aid. A taxi braked and swerved to miss her and a bus coming from the other way actually caught her hand a glancing blow. Then she was on the other side, and the men were grouped around Jamie, who lay on the ground, and she just heard the tallest one say something to him.

"A run isn't over, sonny, until you get back with the money."

Then she was pushing past them and they were fading from the scene and Jamie was sitting up cursing because he couldn't find his shoe and she was there kneeling beside him.

"Oh Jamie, Jamie, what have they done to you? Are you all right?"

He looked at her, his mouth dripping blood and a nasty bruise bleeding slightly on his left cheek.

"I'll get help," she said, beginning to get to her feet. "The police."

But Jamie gripped her wrist to stop her moving. "You'll do nothing. Just nothing. See?"

"But you're hurt, bleeding."

"I'm all right. Just find my bloody shoe, that's all I ask."

Silently Carol picked it up, and watched nervously as Jamie dusted himself down and fingered his wounds. He took the shoe without a word and they walked out of the alley into the road. Mutely, each nursing wounds, they made their way towards the river.

Carol glanced at Jamie out of the corner of her eye. She had never seen him look so dispirited. His hair was matted, his face stained with sweat, dust and blood, his jacket filthy and his collar apparently torn. But worse was the absence of the real Jamie—there was no life in the eye, no jaunty bounce in the step and no words to explain that it was exactly as he had planned, really. In a way, this was a new Jamie, and she longed to reach out to him and help. Suddenly he was both less and more accessible. The communication of words had broken down, but the communication of need had taken over. She felt that perhaps now she could get through to Jamie, but she didn't know how to begin. Instinctively, she adopted her usual role with him.

"It's silly, I know," she said, her words sounding very loud after the silence, "but somehow I feel as if it's all my fault."

Jamie looked straight ahead.

"Don't be so stupid."

For a minute or two they walked silently again.

"I'm sorry," Carol said at last.

No comment.

"I want to help. But I don't know what to do."

Jamie shot her a brief, baleful glance.

"You can't *do* anything."

Carol, encouraged that he had at least broken his silence, plunged into the thing she had been waiting to say.

"But what's the use of . . . loving someone, so much, if you can't help them when they need it. And how can you help them if you don't understand what's really wrong?"

"Who says anything's wrong?"

They walked on for a moment while Carol tried to think of an answer. Then Jamie added an afterthought.

"And what do you mean, 'Don't understand'? If there's something you don't understand, why don't you shut up about it instead of going on saying 'I don't understand, I don't understand.' Of *course* you don't understand. How could you?"

"But I want to understand."

"And suppose I don't want you to?"

"But why not?"

Jamie hesitated a moment.

"Because I made a fool of myself, that's why."

This sudden honesty took Carol by surprise. For the second time she could think of nothing to say.

"I borrowed this money, you see."

"Those men lent you money, Jamie?"

"No, they didn't exactly lend it to me. They didn't know I'd borrowed it. That is, I thought they didn't know."

"But that's stealing."

"Grow up. Anyway, I was going to give it back . . . in the end. What do you think I am, dishonest or something?"

"No."

"Well then?"

"Sometimes you . . . sort of make up your own rules, that's all."

Jamie fell silent again. He took a quick glance at Carol. If he told her he'd borrowed the Crown jewels and was going to put them back on pay day she'd believe him. You couldn't get round it, girls are funny . . . especially Carol. He decided that it might be worth attempting an explanation for her benefit.

"Listen. I delivered something for this man and I got paid for the goods, just like a salesman. I was going to take the money back tonight—you saw me, when I met those men. But in between I'd tried to turn it over—you know, make myself a bit on the side. And the man whose money it was found out. That's all."

Carol, whose spirits rose and fell with Jamie's sun, was suddenly almost elated. Never before had he taken her into his confidence, never before bothered to explain anything except his future schemes. She looked up at him and she was sure he'd hear the pleasure catch in her throat.

"Well, Jamie, if you don't think you did anything wrong . . ."

"Who said anything about doing anything wrong? I said I made a fool of myself. That's different, isn't it?"

Carol looked at him, trying not to grin with satisfaction.

"Next time, I'll know better," he added, taking her hand and swinging it confidentially. "It doesn't pay to be so honest with some people."

Carol couldn't restrain herself any longer. It was joy, it was the oldest game in the world, it was relief and it was very very funny, that last, priceless, only-Jamie-could-have-said-it remark. So she laughed, and her eyes danced, and the lights on the embankment touched her ordinary yellow hair and made it burning gold. And at that moment Jamie decided that he might as well make something out of his defeated day.

"I don't see anything to laugh at," he said, but he put his arm round her waist, and she touched her head on his shoulder, and they strolled even slower and very closely, and both of them laughing: Carol for what had happened, and Jamie because of what he expected to happen, later on.

It was quiet in the mews, in the moonlight, in the shadows; very quiet, not fifty yards from the Cromwell Road and the traffic still rumbling, although it was nearly midnight. So quiet, in fact, that whispers and giggles from Mrs Burry's pretentious front door porch echoed around the whitewashed walls.

"Why can't I stay here, then?" Jamie asked, pinning Carol against the door.

She laid a finger on his lips.

"You know why. Mrs Burry."

Jamie screwed up his face.

"But I don't want to be alone, not tonight."

Carol looked at him, soft and wide-eyed. He pulled her closer, and she came, but turned her head away as he tried to kiss her.

"No Jamie, not out here."

"Where, then? You won't let me in."

"How can I?"

He leaned back a little, and assumed a slightly hurt tone.

"You could, if you wanted to. But that's it, isn't it? You don't want to, not really. Mrs Burry's just a very convenient excuse, isn't she?"

"But Jamie, you know she sleeps right there, in the front room."

Once again Jamie pulled her close to him, playing carefully, gentle and reassuring.

"Look," he whispered in her ear, "I don't want to do anything you don't want to. I just want to be with you, that's all. We can sit and talk, and just . . . well, be together."

Carol pulled back to open her purse and get out the key.

"All right. But—just talk!" Cautiously she opened the door. "And for pete's sake be *quiet*."

The advice was sound and the need obvious. The stairs which they had to ascend were right next to the room where Mrs Burry slept. On the other hand, the breathing which issued from that alcove, rich and fruity, went a long way to covering up any rival sounds of the night.

Despite the precaution of removing his shoes, Jamie managed to penetrate the sound barrier. A stair squeaked loudly. The sleeping beauty stirred, turned, spoke.

"That you, Carol?"

Carol and Jamie froze.

"Yes. Goodnight."

A muffled moan from the bed could have been a reply, or just an incoherent protest. Within seconds the stertorous breathing resumed, and Carol and Jamie covered the last few stairs deftly to reach the refuge of the bedroom.

Carol switched on the lamp on her dressing table. The

room was little more than an attic, but what the West End agents call 'interesting'. Bare rafters cut across the ceiling, and the low windows and alcove seat gave it an intensely feminine feel. At least, it would have been hard to imagine a man living there.

Jamie walked over to the window and drew the curtains. Carol switched on the light. For a moment they regarded each other silently, Jamie with one knee on the window seat, Carol leaning back against the door, smiling but a bit uneasy.

She remembered the last time they had been alone in this room, not long after they had first met. He had been friendly and attentive and amusing, and then started mucking about, apparently just in fun. But suddenly he had become excited and demanding, and before she had had time to think they were on the bed. She had actually bitten his ear and also stuck her finger in his eye; and he had not spoken to her for a fortnight afterwards.

When Carol thought about it, she could not find any really convincing reason for refusing to let Jamie go to bed with her. They were going steady, she liked him—*loved* him, there was no doubt in her mind about that, and she didn't have any particular religious beliefs or moral code to prevent her doing it. The girls at work, in fact, found it hard to believe she didn't. But deep down, implanted, she suspected, by good Aunt Sarah long ago, was a strong feeling that to let Jamie make love to her would be a sell-out to a second best. For her, it would be such a big, big thing—the biggest and most important thing she had ever done. For him, it would be just another minor conquest, to be related over a half pint in the college bar at lunch the next day—and probably the end of anything real between them.

Jamie sat down on the window seat and picked up one of his shoes by the lace.

"Come here, little bird," he whispered.

She watched him, but did not move. This was the same game, she knew that, but now it was all more serious, playing for high stakes.

Jamie let the lace slip slowly through his fingers, his eyes cheeky and staring at her. For a moment Carol envisaged the shoe falling to the floor, the awful thud, and the inevitable effect upon Mrs Burry, sleeping directly below them.

"No!" she hissed, darting across the room to catch it. But it was she who was caught. Jamie half stood up, and grabbed her, pulling her gently but firmly on to the window seat and kissing her so hard his teeth hurt her lips. For a moment she let herself relax, very happy to be held tightly and wanted and caressed. Then she pulled her head back.

"Jamie . . ."

"You've been wonderful tonight, Carol. I don't know what I'd have done if you hadn't been there."

Jamie's voice was soft but urgent, passionate not with sincerity but with desire. He knew even better than Carol what her needs were, what words would stir her and remove the last fragile barrier between wanting and having. And for a moment he seemed to have succeeded.

"Jamie," she said again, softly and with almost pathetic tenderness.

He drew her close again and they kissed. Carol responded, her hand behind his neck pulling his head even closer, her body almost imperceptibly moulding itself against his.

"Carol, Carol," he murmured, "I need you . . ."

She shut her eyes, happy but afraid . . . and felt his hand on her thigh. The spell broke.

"No!" The cry was not a call for help but a plain, clear statement. Suddenly she had made up her mind, seen the truth of the situation. Nothing had altered—least of all Jamie—and she had nearly done that big, big thing, nearly sold out for a few breathy compliments and a little kindness. It was only a statement, but the anguish of decision made it almost a scream.

For a moment the house was silent. Jamie still held her, his face angry and scornful, but they were both stiff and tense.

"What's going on up there?"

Mrs Burry's voice filtered through the floorboards.

"Now look what you've done, little Miss Virginity!" Jamie hissed at her. "What's with you, I'd like to know?"

"I'm sorry . . ."

Carol shook her head, looking at him with eyes rapidly filling with tears. She didn't want to lose him, and yet both ways that seemed to be her destiny. As Mrs Burry's footsteps creaked on the stairs, they pulled apart.

"I'm sorry . . ." Carol said again, as Jamie pulled back the curtain and opened the window.

"Lot of good *that* is!" he said, climbing on to the sill, and sitting astride the frame—he had no stomach for facing angry landladies at something past midnight in single girls' bedrooms.

He was just about to swing the other leg over when Mrs Burry opened the door. For one infinitely long second they surveyed each other: Jamie poised uncertainly against the night sky, Mrs Burry (enjoying it) leaning on the door post, her house-coat not properly buttoned up and her hair in curlers.

"Leaving?" she enquired.

Jamie tried to take it in his stride. He swung a leg casually back into the room and stood by the window seat uncertainly.

"Come on, Batman," said Mrs Burry, indicating the stairway with her thumb. Jamie crossed the room slowly, his face a mixture of contempt, anger and embarrassment. He did not even give Carol a glance. As he passed Mrs Burry, she could not resist turning the knife in the wound.

"If you don't know the rules, you shouldn't play."

"Rules?" His pent up anger exploded in the word. "You women are always going on about rules." He pushed past her.

Mrs Burry addressed his back as he descended the stairs.

"There's only one. Don't get caught." She turned to Carol. "And you'd better watch your step, young lady, or out you go, too."

As she shut the door behind her, Carol stood without moving. She heard the front door slam. If Jamie was gone—gone for good—then this was the most awful moment of her life. She had hurt his pride, she realised that. Where Jamie was concerned, it would be better even to have hurt his pocket. Probably he would never come near her again . . . and yet, only half an hour ago, they had seemed so close, closer than ever. It was all too cold and bitter for tears, but she felt sick.

A pebble hit the window pane. Carol turned, listened. Again there was the rattle. Her face lit up and she made it to the window in two strides. She pushed it open and leant out. Sure enough, there was Jamie below, looking up. Perhaps after all . . .

Jamie made a furious but silent gesture. She stared at him hopefully.

"I want my coat, that's all," he said in a harsh stage whisper. "Throw it down."

Carol fetched it and threw it to him.

"Jamie . . ." she began to say. But he turned on his heel, without even waiting to put it on, and stormed out of the mews.

3

It was all happening outside, in the hot streets, pavements scorching the soles of your shoes, crowds pushing and traffic hazy through diesel fumes and heat.

DRINKA PINTA MORE
COME CO-OPERATIVE SHOPPING
DOUBLE DIAMOND WORKS WONDERS
BILLY'S BACK

It was all happening outside, on the sides of the buses, in the lunch-time scramble. There was another war just started, men dying, blood flowing, tanks like scorched memorials in the sand. In the world of men there were murders and Test matches and Cabinet crises. It was all happening, everywhere but here.

Carol looked up at the bare walls, the sun baking them white against the incredibly blue sky, and sighed. The more it happened out there, the more it seemed dead in here, like a barren island, another world, a kind of desert. The church was in the middle of it all, but it had no part in it. Samuel Sebastian Grey slept on beneath her feet, even if Billy was back.

Which reminded her. She felt in her pocket and found Aunt Sarah's letter, creased but intact.

"You really ought to go and hear this Billy Graham," it said, towards the end, after Topsy's chill and the problem of the birds who drink the morning milk. "I think you'd find him interesting. Earls Court is very near your lodgings, isn't it? Why don't you go along, and then write and tell me what you thought of it?"

Billy Graham! Carol pulled a face. Imagine what Jamie would make of that.

Which also reminded her. Jamie. It didn't really seem to matter much any more what he thought, about Billy Graham

33

or anything else. Ever since that awful evening—Jamie storming out of the mews—he had disappeared. Three days. Three lunch hours. She worked it out: 105 minutes in this weird place, counting the flagstones and feeding the sparrows with cheese sandwiches. How many more days would she come here before hope died out, hope that he would just appear, bouncy and confident, acting as though nothing had happened?

She looked at the sparrows and dropped a large morsel in the middle of the scrum. After all, they came each day on the off-chance of a bit of bread from her bag. She supposed they even turned up on Saturdays and Sundays. Unless sparrows could count. Or had calendars.

Carol laughed out loud, and the more nervous birds flew away. But within a minute they were back in the melee, pecking away as though they hadn't been feeding luxuriously now for three sickening days. If the birds could turn up here, in this overgrown place of death, day in and day out—and even on Sundays—then she reckoned she could keep it up a bit longer.

Of course, if she were somebody else—Diana, for instance —she would phone him up. But what would she say? "I'm so sorry I wouldn't let you seduce me the other night. It'll be all right next time. When can we meet?" In fact, she wasn't sorry—not about that. And it would be just the same the next time, and the time after that. As for meeting, at the best of times she hoped and waited, and he turned up if there wasn't anything more important to do.

She wished she could hate him. But even thinking about how unreasonable he was made her want to see him, with a sort of empty ache in her stomach. It wasn't like he said— "If you loved me, you wouldn't mind". How wrong can you be? It was just the opposite. It was because she loved him so much that she did mind, desperately.

But he would never understand. Not Jamie.

The real question was, should it have a top or not? Jamie pencilled in a low cut line, grimaced, and changed it into a lace edged eighteenth century sort of neck. Finally he gave the face a beard, added a pair of George Woodcock eyebrows and a Jimmy Hendrix hair-do, and sat back to survey the general effect. Stunning. Jamie felt that Algernon, rattling on up there about the tensile properties of pre-stressed rayon, could learn a few things from this angle.

He caught Sid's eye. Time for an intervention. This one had gone on long enough.

"Excuse me, sir."

Algernon Clare stopped in mid-stream, slipped his glasses on and identified the source of the sound.

"Yes Hopkins?"

"Well, sir, I was wondering whether this pre-stressed rayon had ever been used in the lingerie field?"

The class sat up, interested. Several were grinning already, knowing Jamie. Others relaxed, the flow of knowledge having stopped, and wriggled their numb extremities on the hard school chairs.

"Lingerie? Well yes. I suppose so." Clare paused, sensing the air of mischief in the room. "Hopkins, I am well aware that my knowledge of pre-stressed rayon cannot equal your knowledge of ladies' lingerie. But I must remind you that this is my lecture, that the subject is the one on your time-table, and that most of us have no time for adolescent jokes about underwear."

There was a rapt silence. First round to Clare, it seemed. The lecturer certainly thought so, smiling rather smugly at the middle distance. All eyes were on Jamie. He was smiling too.

"It was only that it occurred to me," he said, ignoring Clare's last remarks completely, "that pre-stressed rayon might solve a serious problem for a lady friend of mine in Soho." He paused while the class waited for the pay-off. "Her G-string shrinks when it's damp."

Clare bravely weathered the class's exaggerated roar of delight, contenting himself with an observation to the effect that they did not often have the pleasure of Hopkins' company at their lectures, and now they knew where he was spending the time. But the damage was done. Every subsequent reference to pre-stressed rayon was greeted with guffaws and the class broke up for coffee ten minutes early.

As Jamie was pushing his way through the crowd to the door, Sid caught his arm.

"Hey, Jamie. What about that ten bob you owe me? I thought I'd ask before you shot off to the Pigalle again."

Jamie stopped, and looked serious.

"Look, things are tight this week, Sid. My mother's off sick again—I've had to pay the rent. You know how it is with a state grant. I mean, if you're really stuck for a couple of bob . . ."

"No. Forget it. When you can."

Jamie grinned wanly, brave through adversity.

"Thanks mate—do the same for you some time."

One minor skirmish out of the way, he tried again to reach the exit. He made it, but no further, for Mr Baker, the college bursar, blocked his path.

"Ah, Hopkins," he said, like a man coming upon a long lost quarry. "I've been wanting to see you. I'd like an explanation."

Jamie dropped his voice.

"I'll be in your office first thing in the morning, Mr Baker."

"That's all I've heard from you for weeks. You are now a whole term in arrears with your tuition fees . . . and the cheque you gave me bounced."

"A mistake, I assure you. I have taken it up with the bank manager."

"Nonsense."

The word came out crisp and clean, like a torpedo from a submarine. The sheer, crude clarity of it shook Jamie. For once he was lost for words.

"Nonsense, Hopkins. I talked with your bank, and learnt that your account was closed three days before the date on your cheque." Still Jamie was speechless. "I have had enough of pursuing you for money. There is a waiting list for places at this college, and one of them will become vacant shortly if those fees are not paid in full, and without my having to ask you again."

The verbal victory in the lecture room seemed hours ago. Angry, embarrassed and afraid, Jamie decided on flight.

"Well, I'm sorry. I can't do anything about it just this minute. I'll see you tomorrow."

As he made off, Baker called after him, "Be sure you do, that's all. I've given you fair warning."

Sid, who was passing, stopped.

"Go easy on him, Mr Baker," he said. "He's got problems. His mother's off sick again."

"Really? How strange." Baker was taken aback. "Why on earth didn't he tell me?"

On the steps of the college Jamie paused, and then set off through the afternoon crowds, destination undecided. There was no doubt about his most pressing need—cash. And that meant Fitch, and all the problem of getting around the events of three days ago. Pressing as the need was, he wasn't sure that he could cope with the situation in the aftermath of his brush with Baker. First, he must get in the mood.

Which probably meant Barry and Swallow's. He was too late to catch Carol at the church—it never occurred to him that she might not have kept tryst there—but he could pop into the millinery department, provided that old bag of a superviser wasn't around.

The way he looked at it—threading his way into Oxford Street, grinning at the girl in the Chicken Inn, half way through her mixed grill at the table in the window—Carol owed him an apology. But she couldn't very well apologise to him if she never saw him, and so, being a reasonable sort of bloke, the least he could do was to give her the opportunity. He was not inclined to be toffee-nosed about it. A gesture was called for, and he was prepared to make it.

Of course, he could have had her the other night. If it hadn't been for Mrs Burry, that 'no' would have changed into 'yes please' within seconds. It stood to reason. She worshipped the ground he trod on. She looked at him—in company, too—in a strange, embarrassing way. She was potty about him. He could do anything with her. Except, of course, this . . . so far.

It wasn't that he was a sex maniac or something, who couldn't think about anything else. In fact, he liked Carol. The last couple of days, if he was honest, he'd missed her. But if she loved him she shouldn't mind, that was his point.

So he'd give her a chance to apologise, and then they'd be back like they were before, with her neat and warm and around when he needed her. He looked at his watch. But not now. The warm sun, the stroll, the silently smooth cameras which had slowly moved into position, closer as his spirits rose: now he was ready for Fitch, ready for anything.

Carol kicked off her shoes under the counter and stood on tiptoe a moment to rest her heels. Thank heaven it was the last day of the sale. It looked like it, too, with piles of boxes everywhere, tempers a bit short, and no bargains left—just the hats that got left at every sale, and brought out again (dusted, re-priced) at the next one. The last of the late lunchers were just mauling her way through the fifteen bob pile and then—Carol glanced up at the clock—five minutes to a cup of tea.

This particular late luncher was rather a giggle, Carol decided. Either she was the world's worst shopper or else her mind wasn't on the job. She'd picked up that straw boater three times already, and kept making as if to come over to the counter. But each time she glanced at Carol, blushed, and put it down again.

She was an odd-looking girl, too. You couldn't pin it down to details, but there was a built-in incongruity in her appearance. The clothes, taken one at a time, were presentable and reasonably in touch. Her hair, short and casual, was exactly like half the other girls who swarmed over the store in the lunch hour. Her face was interesting: not exactly ugly, but bony, disjointed, apparently made up of unrelated pieces put together. That was it. Clothes, hair, face, even her walk—she was a sort of spare parts person. Carol began to award marks to the parts: eyes—good, say seven; nose—sharp, pointed, four; legs—too long, but shaped well, five; hands—big, raw fingers, two.

She stopped abruptly, because the late luncher was almost upon her, clutching the straw boater but still looking as indecisive as ever.

"I think ... er, yes, this one. Please."

But she smiled at Carol, and that was a warm, friendly, open one; eight, possibly nine, out of ten.

Carol took it, removed the price tag, and accepted a pound note.

"You took a while making up your mind," she said.

"Oh dear, yes. I do . . . I mean, always. Well, it's fifteen shillings, isn't it? It's a bargain, I know, but I still don't like . . . well . . . wasting money." She paused, but Carol made no move to speak. In fact, she was spell-bound by the customer's eyes, which were larger than she had realised, and green. She marked them up to eight.

The late luncher mistook her silence for disagreement, and reinforced her argument.

"I mean, there's so much your money can do, people starving, orphans, the homeless . . . Well, it seems wrong to waste it."

Carol grinned suddenly.

"Sure you really want it?"

"Oh yes. Yes. I've made up my mind. Though I may regret it tomorrow. I usually do."

She picked up the hat and her change, and turned to go. Carol saw two coloured tickets on the spot where the late luncher's handbag had stood, and called after her. "Oh miss, you've left something . . ."

The customer turned, and her face was scarlet with embarrassment.

"I thought they might be yours," Carol said. "Fallen out of your purse."

She picked them up and saw that they were tickets for Billy Graham at Earls Court (The GREATER LONDON CRUSADE, it said).

"Actually, I'm sort of . . . spreading them about. I mean, if you're free tomorrow evening . . . It's really very interesting, you know."

Carol felt for her. She guessed what it was costing her, poor girl. All her life, probably: teased on the hockey field, left like a wall-flower at the school dances, butt of the vulgar set in the typing pool. And now, to stand there and tell a complete stranger about Billy Graham at Earls Court. Carol hadn't the heart to say 'no', just like that.

"I can't say for sure, but I might be able to use them," she said. "Thanks, anyway."

As the late luncher smiled with relief and made at top speed for the exit, Carol remembered who it was she reminded her of. She should have got it right away, of course— it was the eyes, and the spare parts. Aunt Sarah.

Jamie pushed open the door of Fitch's shop. The bell jangled, and again he felt his stomach muscles go tense. He had felt all right until he got in sight of the shop, and then his nerve began to fail him. It was one thing to walk through the crowds and play a scene to your own script, meeting every one of Fitch's sinister remarks with a witty deflection, master of the situation, cool, impudent, confident. It was quite another to be going into his shop three days after you'd tried to turn his money over, and got yourself roughed up by his play-mates in the process.

He pushed the door shut, and again the bell jangled. From the back room Hubert and Fitch appeared, the mask of well-bred civility ("Good morning, my Lord. I trust her ladyship is well and enjoying the season?") disintegrating the moment Fitch recognised Jamie.

"I thought you'd show up, Hopkins."

Fitch slowly opened his gold case and began to light one of his elegant black cigarettes.

At once, Jamie's confidence returned. Fitch could not have done more to set him at ease. Suddenly they were back in the 'B' movie, a world in which Jamie was completely at home. It was the real world that bothered him, not suave master crooks with elegant black cigarettes and silk dressing gowns.

"Now you wouldn't think much of me if I didn't profit by my mistakes, would you Mr Fitch?"

Fitch made a nonchalant pass with his cigarette.

"You're wasting my time, Hopkins."

"I mean, we can all learn something, can't we?"

Fitch glanced at Hubert, who stood impassively behind the counter. Then he narrowed his eyes slightly and dropped his voice.

"I'm afraid it wouldn't be easy for you to prove that I can trust you again. I doubt if you'd be prepared to do what I have in mind."

(Jamie could hardly believe it. They were using his script.)

"Of course," Fitch continued, "It could be a very lucrative arrangement."

The silently smooth cameras moved into position. This was too good to be true. Jamie controlled his excitement, playing the situation, cool, impudent, confident.

"Try me and see."

Again Fitch glanced at Hubert.

"I want the key to the office where your mother works."

The cameras disappeared. Ruby Hopkins was back in the real world; why were they bringing her into the picture? Suddenly they'd left the script, and Jamie was momentarily speechless.

"My mother? What one earth for?"

Fitch studied Jamie's face, speaking quietly, but so that every word sank in.

"The psychiatrist she works for, Berman—he's a top man. He's experimenting with psychedelic drugs."

"Happy pills?"

"No. Mind expanders. On our market they're like diamonds."

Unbelief, shock, amazement chased each other across Jamie's face. All this time he'd been short of a quid or two, and he'd been within knocking distance of Fort Knox. He tried to get his mind back on the script, but it wouldn't work. Dimly he was aware of Fitch and Hubert standing there, grinning at him, enjoying his reaction. He wanted to ask them how they knew, and what else they knew that he didn't. But it was dawning on him that he had badly underestimated Fitch. He was playing in Division One now.

"What's in it for me?" he asked at last.

"A fair share."

Jamie thought a moment.

"You know, it might not be as easy as all that."

"In that case, forget it." Fitch knew when a catch was really hooked.

"But I'll think of a way."

Fitch half turned towards his back room, the interview clearly at an end.

"I'm sure you will, Hopkins," he said quietly.

Four days. Four hot, miserable days, four lost lunch-hours, and four restless nights. Carol hurled a crust at the sparrows and totted up the damage. She had a splitting head-ache, she had laddered her stocking on the corrugated iron entrance and the sun on the stone walls and on her head was like a great, oppressive weight.

Of course, the sparrows were still there, faithful even on Saturdays and Sundays, kicking up the dust and worrying the life out of the last cheese sandwich. And Samuel Sebastian Grey was there, too, underneath her feet, his works still following him.

But no Jamie. And seeing it was now ten past one, it looked like being five days.

Or for ever. She refused to face it, but the fact was they had had a terrible row and Jamie had stormed out of the mews, face like thunder. She couldn't apologise, because she wasn't sorry, except at annoying him; and he wouldn't apologise, because she'd hurt his pride more than anything else.

A shadow fell across the flag-stone in front of her.

"Can't think what you see in those stupid birds . . ."

She jumped up—surprise, joy—and knocked the bag of sandwiches upside down. For a moment she stood there, happy, and yet not quite sure how he wanted it played, wait-ing for a clue. Jamie stooped down and picked up the sand-wich bag, peering inside and selecting one that had not dusted itself on the ground. Then he sat down and took a bite.

"They haven't got any sense and they're not even pretty."

Carol relaxed. It was going to be as though nothing had ever happened. No apologies. No explanations. She sat down beside him, and also took a sandwich.

"I like them. I understand them."

"What is there to understand?"

Carol thought a moment.

"If I was a bird, I'd probably be a sparrow."

They both laughed. Jamie needed this, after Baker, and Fitch, and the news about his mother's office. He didn't mind Carol looking at him like that in here, with no-one about.

42

In fact, if she weren't so fussy he'd show her right now what looking at a man like that was all about.

There was a broken off pillar by the overgrown aisle, about six or seven feet high. While Carol tried to brush grass and dirt off a cucumber sandwich, Jamie scaled it and sat himself on the top.

"What are you doing up there?" she asked him, half turning.

"Keeping my distance. That's what you want, isn't it?"

Carol laughed, because he was smiling, but it reminded her of the shadows and she became uncertain for a moment, not sure how to play it from there.

But Jamie changed the tune again.

"What shall we do tonight, then?"

Carol hesitated. "Well, I didn't know I'd be seeing you."

"Why, you got something planned?"

"Not really. I mean, it doesn't matter. There was this customer—a girl—gave me two tickets for tonight. I thought Mrs Burry might go with me."

Jamie nodded wisely. "Clever. Getting in her good books again."

"Well, I didn't want to go on my own."

"What are they for?"

"Earls Court—you know, Billy Graham."

Jamie nearly fell off the pillar with simulated mirth.

"Mrs Burry, going to hear Billy Graham!" He thought for a second. "Now, if you took Billy Graham to hear Mrs Burry, you might have something. He could learn a thing or two from her."

"I don't have to go," Carol said, defensively.

"Tell you what. Why don't we go together? It might be good for a giggle."

"I'd like to. Aunt Sarah said I ought to go and hear him." Jamie looked serious.

"Let's get it straight. I'm going for the laughs, that's all. This religion kick gives me the creeps. I mean, it's not as though he's selling anything new, is it? Beats me why they all flock to hear him."

"Perhaps he says things people want to hear."

"What—like give up sex, lay off the bottle, go to church

43

on Sundays? You must be kidding. No, it isn't what you sell, it's how you sell it that counts. I might pick up a few tips along that line, you never know."

"Shall I meet you there, then?"

"No—I'll call for you," Jamie jumped down from the pillar, frightening the sparrows.

"You won't be late?"

Jamie dusted his hands and laughed.

"Who, me? You must be thinking of someone else."

4

Jamie glanced at his watch, and accelerated. He should have been at Carol's at seven, and now it was ten past.

But he'd done a really good day's work since lunch time. He felt the key in his pocket, passport to Eldorado, and grinned to himself. It had been easy, like taking sweets from a nipper.

First he'd sussed the place. His mum had been quite taken aback to see him walk into the surgery, large as life. Fitch was right, it was a classy pad: period furniture, gold-framed mirrors, fitted carpets, that sort of thing. Obviously his mother was well in—the way the doctor let her go early just because he'd shown up, and the fact that she had a front door key.

That had been easy, too. He'd watched her put it in her hand-bag, and borrowed it while she was frying his kipper for tea. Then a quick dash round the corner to the iron-monger's—keys made while you wait—and the original was back in her bag before she'd had a chance to miss it.

It was then, about half past five, that he'd decided to change the plan. There was the key in his hand—all done by kindness—and cabinets full of priceless pills at Dr Berman's place. Now why should Fitch be the one to cash in?

This had to be thought through, but the principle was clear. Hopkins takes the risks, Hopkins has the contacts at Berman's, Hopkins uses his contacts to get the key. And then, the whole thing set up, Fitch and Hubert pop along and fill their sacks with presents. The sheer injustice of it choked him.

He had told Fitch that he'd learnt from his past mistakes. He had, indeed. He'd learnt that with people like Fitch you couldn't be too careful. They had spies everywhere. So you trusted nobody and did it all yourself.

The trouble was, he couldn't get rid of the stuff. For that, you needed a market—someone like Jenkins. Jamie fingered the fading bruise on his cheek thoughtfully. He couldn't trust Jenkins, that was the fly in the ointment. The Jenkins bit would need careful handling, but if he'd got the pills he was sure ordinary greed would do the trick.

He hadn't fancied the thought of breaking into Berman's surgery. It was risky, and he wouldn't know what to look for when he'd got in. At a bit after six-thirty the major refinement of the plan occurred to him. He'd looked up Berman's phone number and called him from a kiosk. He was rather pleased at the way he had handled what could have been the trickiest part of all.

"This is Jamie Hopkins," he had said, "Mrs Hopkins' son. Excuse my ringing you so late, but there's rather an urgent matter I'd like to discuss with you. It's difficult to go into on the phone, but . . ."

And there and then Berman had agreed to see him during his mother's lunch break the next day, as he'd rather she didn't know about it, "no point in causing her extra worry". It had all gone rather well, and Berman sounded a nice, friendly, trusting sort of sucker.

But all this hard work had made him a bit late for Carol, which was a pity, but not too serious because she would wait. She always did.

Mrs Burry looked at herself in Carol's mirror. Not bad, not bad at all. The old brown dress—'Burry's boggler', Alf used to call it—still did something for her, and if the light wasn't too bright and her mascara didn't melt, the general effect was all right. She felt quite excited, just like old times, Waterloo under the clock and a young corporal waiting for her.

Some people would think it was kinky, she supposed. But she liked them young, uniforms still new, arms and hands strong and voices excited because it's all happening, and there isn't much time to be choosy. Ever since the War, she'd never been able to stomach these fat men with receding hair, the ones she'd been to school with, but now they looked past it, their breath stale and their eyes dull.

And Carol could spare her this one, for tonight. In any case, the girl didn't know what it was all about, just a kid, really. No idea how to make a boy feel grown up and manly. She patted her hair. They wouldn't need to go out into the black-out. Just a nice evening together, a bottle of sherry, perhaps, and if the bombs started up they could keep warm and safe in the alcove under the stairs.

She heard Jamie whistle outside, and opened the door. Jamie was in and on the first stair before she could say anything.

"Carol left some time ago."

That stopped him in his tracks.

"Where did she go?"

"How do I know," said Mrs Burry, looking in the mirror and touching her hair. "She doesn't tell me everything."

"That's funny." Jamie looked genuinely puzzled.

"Well, there's a first time for everything. Young girls are a selfish lot."

'Not Carol." Jamie was surprised to hear himself defending her.

"I think she went off to meet someone. It sounded like a theatre date. 'By the box office', she said."

Jamie hesitated at the foot of the stairs, unwilling to accept the fact of Carol's absence. It was all so out of character. He was vaguely aware of Mrs Burry eyeing him and pouring out two glasses of sherry.

"No consideration, these bits of girls," she said sadly. "Don't know how to treat a feller. Lack of experience, that's it of course."

Jamie had a sudden thought.

"Perhaps she left a note," he said, and darted up the stairs two at a time.

Mrs Burry watched him go. There wasn't any note, she knew that. "Tell Jamie I've gone to get a bite to eat and I'll see him there, by the main box office." That's what she'd said. It wouldn't do her any harm to kick her heels for a couple of hours, little miss purity. Some people didn't know their luck, with nice, strong young men, fresh and excited, calling for them. She could make room tonight for someone who did.

Jamie came down, rather more slowly.

"Maybe you don't know her as well as you think," Mrs Burry said darkly.

He rejected the idea with vigour, obviously wrong-footed. "I know her. Know all about her." He stepped towards the door.

Mrs Burry seized her moment, heart pounding, eyes appealing for consent.

"No need to rush off. Have a drink. I'll show you my medal."

Jamie looked at her, as though seeing her for the first time. He suddenly realised she was dressed up and wearing her war paint, presumably for him. But she must have been every day of forty-five, the same age as his mother. It was weird, kinky, like something in a modern play. He watched her warily.

"Don't tell me you don't know all about it," she said, her voice thick. "I've seen the way you look at her. You can't get it there, can you? Well, now's your chance."

At that moment Jamie saw the funny side of it—her stood there, like mutton dressed up as lamb, clutching two glasses of sherry; and him an innocent lad, pretending he didn't know what she was on about. He grinned.

"Not tonight, Luv. I'm trying to give it up."

Mrs. Burry put the glasses down, and tried the other tack.

"What's the matter—scared? That's it, isn't it? Just a frightened little boy who rings doorbells and runs away."

Jamie thought of door-bells he had rung, and grinned again. He raised his hand and imitated a bell ringing.

"Ah well," he said, "Ting-a-ling!"

As the door slammed behind him, the whistle of a train sounded, and there were young men in uniform everywhere, and one waving to her through the steam, and the carriage moving and tears on her cheeks. It would all be all right after the War, he had said. But there wasn't any after, not then, not now and not ever.

Jamie sat on the platform at Earls Court, sandwiched between two parsons and not ten feet from Billy Graham himself. He felt rather pleased with the achievement and

48

hoped that, wherever Carol was sitting in the crowded arena (as he had no doubt she was), she would see him and be suitably impressed.

It was the doorman's fault, really. He shouldn't have been so stroppy when Jamie arrived without a ticket. He wouldn't listen to his explanation and simply told him to get on the end of the queue for unreserved seats, which was about half a mile long. That might be all right for the serfs, but Jamie had no intention of being shut out of a religious jamboree when he had in the past gate-crashed celebrity dances and a film star's wedding. By comparison, this was dead easy.

A quick reccy revealed the VIP door round the side. Tagging alongside a slightly confused elderly clergyman, whom Jamie engaged in animated conversation, he had walked straight in under the nose of a uniformed attendant and then left the poor old boy as suddenly as he had joined him.

Inside, it was a bit like the circus. There were people rushing backwards and forwards, stalls selling hotdogs and ice creams, and bookstands selling what Jamie discovered, to his horror, were religious papers and magazines. From the arena came the sound of a large choir singing, their voices echoing around the outer area, blurring the noise of footsteps, the shouting and the clatter of the escalators.

The distinctive thing was the air of dedication everywhere. About half the people Jamie saw seemed to be wearing large badges—STEWARD, COUNSELLOR, ADVISOR, CHOIR—all in different colours. There appeared to be a preponderance of single ladies, serious of face, intent of purpose, hurrying in all directions. But there were also, Jamie was relieved to note, a good number of mini-skirted younger women and even a few modish young men in the correct gear.

Jamie grabbed the arm of a perspiring gentleman with glasses, who was wearing a large badge marked STEWARD.

"Where do I sit?" he asked him.

The steward looked at him warily.

"Ticket?" he enquired, panting slightly, presumably from exertion. It could hardly be religious ecstasy, Jamie decided, at this early stage in the proceedings.

"No. No ticket. I'm with the VIPs."

49

The steward's attitude changed somewhat.

"Well brother," he said—Jamie masked a grin—"The VIP section is round the other side. Unless you're in the platform party?"

Well why not? thought Jamie. Might as well be where the action is.

"Yes, that's it," he said aloud. "The platform. That's what they said on the phone."

The steward was trying to place the face. Not one of the Team, he was sure, but perhaps a guest, from sport—no, not dressed like that—or showbusiness. Yes, that would probably be it.

"For the platform, sir, you go round the side here and in through the wide corner entrance to the arena. You'll have to show the platform pass there, of course."

"Thanks," said Jamie, "Thanks, brother."

He was particularly grateful for the tip off about the platform pass. It gave him a chance to think something up. Just take it easy, that was the trick with this gate-crashing game. Look the part and never panic.

As Jamie entered the arena, he was momentarily taken aback by the sea of faces on all sides, the crowd even filling the floor space. He made his way towards the platform, sauntering jauntily as if he had done it a dozen times before. Obviously the action was up front, and that was where he intended to be. A steward stopped him at the foot of the platform stairs.

"Excuse me. A pass is needed for the platform."

Jamie smiled at him pleasantly.

"Sorry, old chap," he said. "I left it with Allison, of All Saints. He's just coming."

There was enough authority in Jamie's voice to make the steward hesitate, and that was all he needed to navigate the stairs and make it on to the platform. Jamie reckoned that once he was up there, nobody would bother him. With all those news-reel cameras and the Press there in force they wouldn't want a scene. It would look rather bad, whatever way it was reported. Selecting a seat in the front row, Jamie sunk down into it and prepared to enjoy the action.

Carol could hardly believe it. How could even Jamie do it to her After all, it was his suggestion, really, and there was only one main box office. And here it was, seven-thirty and the choir singing inside, and no Jamie. It was her destiny, it seemed, to spend her life waiting for him.

He'd seemed so friendly earlier, too. Surely he couldn't have changed his mind so soon? After all, he'd come to the church looking for her, and he hadn't raised the other matter. Everything had seemed so good and bright half an hour ago, and now it had all clouded over. As the crowd poured in past her, the long queue edging forward, she could have wept for sheer loneliness. She looked at the two tickets in her hand, and thought of the late luncher and Aunt Sarah. There was no point in waiting any longer, and she didn't fancy her bedroom on this of all nights. She turned slowly, casting one last, hopeful look over the mass of people invading the building, and made her way inside.

Carol wasn't sure what she had expected, but it wasn't this. Somehow it was hard to associate Aunt Sarah—village chapel, harmonium, pictures of a blonde and bearded Jesus on the walls—with this. Massed choirs, metallic voices trying to be hearty over a public address system, a negro soloist and all around this vast, silent crowd in an echoing barn of a building. In any case, her mind was full of Jamie. She had just reached the stage—ridiculous as it was, and inevitable—of worrying that he had been knocked down on his way to meet her, and was at this very moment lying on an operating table ... or even in the morgue.

Jamie, on the other hand, knew exactly what he had expected, and it was all running true to form. As he saw it, it was all a great big confidence trick, superbly planned and executed, with a primary aim of getting a good collection (and selling stacks of those books and records they kept on plugging), and a secondary aim of persuading thousands of mugs to join the church. He didn't know what the joining fee was, but obviously Graham got a good cut of it. So far as he could see, everything—the music, the notices, the choir, the slow build-up towards the moment (due now, he reckoned) when Graham got up to speak—was calculated to

51

soften up the customers and make them more ready to part with their cash and, later, sign on the dotted line. It was a good touch having these bishops and parsons on the platform to give the whole thing a respectable air. He wondered what the proles made of him, sitting up there with dog collars all around him.

The whole audience was still and attentive as Billy Graham got up to speak. To Jamie, ten feet away, it was obvious what got the birds. To Carol, at the far end of the arena, he was simply a dark dot in a pool of light from the arcs. He held a large, floppy Bible and wore a neck microphone.

"Many of you here tonight are searching for a purpose and a reason for your existence." The voice was undeniably arresting, sharp, confident. "You're searching for something permanent, something you can hold on to and sink your teeth in, something you can believe.

"Where did I come from? Why am I here? Where am I going?" (You may well ask, thought Jamie.) "Those are questions that young people especially are asking in their most serious moments. That's why tonight, for many of you, will be an hour and a moment that will be historic in your life."

Jamie looked around the arena. Half of them were sunk already, hanging on every word. It was pathetic, really, the way people were like sheep, just waiting for somebody to tell them the way. Any way.

Carol found herself listening, despite her anxieties about Jamie. She wasn't terribly bothered about where she had come from, or even where she was going to; but she did, quite desperately, want to find this "something permanent" Billy Graham had referred to. But he got off on to the intellectual problems of students, and lost her for ten minutes.

He picked her up again, though, when he got on to idols.

"Human beings are, by nature, sinners," he said. "Now that doesn't mean that we are bad all over. That doesn't mean we are all wicked. What it means is that we all have the tendency towards wrong. We all tend to go our own way, rather than God's.

"For instance, the Bible says 'Thou shalt have no other

gods beside me'. That means, nothing and no-one should take the place in our lives that belongs only to God.

"But we all have our idols, our God-substitutes. With some, it's their work or business. With some, it's money. With some, it's their lovely home. With some, it's a person—a husband or wife, a friend or loved one. Human love is very good, but to put a human being in the place that belongs to God is sin."

That was it, thought Carol. There was her problem in a nutshell. Jamie was god to her. He dominated her days and haunted her nights. Without him, the brightest day was dull. With him, anything could be borne. It was crazy, but that shallow, unreliable, selfish young man (she knew him, knew all about him) had become the indispensable centre of her being.

What a load of old toffee, thought Jamie. How does he know it's not the other way round? Perhaps it's God who's a substitute for money, or sex, or success. Looking at some of the drab people in the audience, he reckoned that could be a better explanation.

Graham went on, the arc lights burnishing his hair, exaggerating his lantern jaw and pale, intense face.

"This disease of sin with which we are all infected, that causes people to lie, to cheat, to steal, to lust and to commit immorality . . ."

Jamie grinned knowledgeably. He'd been waiting for that. Sex rears its ugly head. Now prepare to meet thy doom.

"This disease that corrupts men and causes hatred, murder and war, also affects your mind, so that you cannot see God clearly, you cannot understand the Bible, you cannot understand spiritual things.

"But when you receive Christ, by faith, a change takes place in your mind. God says, 'Let there be light!' And immediately the veil is lifted and for the first time you can comprehend something of God.

"In fact, your faith can be very weak. The Bible says that all you need is the faith of a mustard seed, and the mustard seed is so small"—the distant figure hugged itself and drooped its shoulders to capture the smallness of it—'you can hardly see it at all.

"We come to God by faith. Then we begin to reason it out in every way we possibly can, and we can buttress our faith with reason." Slotting gestures of the hand indicated how the faithful could be building their concrete castles of belief.

"To Christians, it's the only thing in the world that makes sense. But before you come to Christ it doesn't make any sense at all. It sounds like rubbish."

You can say that again, thought Jamie. But the audience was intent, still. Pity the bloke hadn't got a better product to sell, because the projection was fantastic.

Graham dropped his voice, adopted a conversational, person-to-person tone.

"You see, you have a body and you have a spirit. But your spirit is dead because of sin. That's why you never find fulfilment in life . . ."

And Carol was hooked, because that was her. It all came back from years ago, with the smell of paraffin lamps on Sunday evenings and Aunt Sarah playing the harmonium. It meant something then, praying and singing hymns and simply believing that God was there and loved her and understood her problems. So what had happened to it all? It had seemed real, but now it was dead and gone. And, true enough, fulfilment had gone with it.

"Jesus said you need to be born again. You need to find new life in Christ."

Graham leant forward over the rostrum, every line of his body tense with the effort of communication.

"It's like finding the key to a jigsaw puzzle. It's finding the key of the Universe. It's finding the key of your life. It's finding that mysterious thing that people are searching for all over the world . . .

"And here comes Jesus Christ, the Son of God, and says, 'I am the truth'. 'Ye shall know the truth and the truth shall set you free!'

"I know it sounds fantastic and ridiculous to say that Jesus Christ, through dying on a cross 1900 years ago, and rising again, can affect me and give me a new life, so that I can face the world with a new resource and a new power and a new dimension of living—and then be assured of life to come. But it's true, and it happens."

Carol was half listening, but most of all she was listening to other voices, from simpler, less complicated days. Yet the new element was the one that had been missing—the reality of it, the blinding light that had just shown her what a shadow person she really was, and what was missing from the core of her personality. Her heart was pounding, her hands were clammy. The clear cut issue resolved itself in her mind. She knew what she had to do, but could she do it? Somehow, if she was ever to be free, if she was ever to be *real*, she had got to dethrone Jamie from his high place in her heart, and give it to God. While Jamie dominated her and filled her thoughts, God and Jesus Christ would never get a look in, and she would never be herself.

"Oh God, help me," she groaned—audibly, she realised, because the woman sitting next to her glanced at her out of the corner of her eye and shifted in her seat.

"I'm not talking about an emotional experience."

Graham's voice intruded again, metallic, sharp. "I'm talking about your mind and your will saying, 'I can love God, I can believe in God, I can serve God. I believe that Christ died for me. I don't understand it all, but I believe it . . .'

"You have to be willing to give up those things that are wrong in your life, the idols, the lying, the cheating, the sex outside marriage . . ."

That's it, thought Carol. Being willing, willing to see Jamie taken away and a God she hardly knew at all take his place. It's all very well to say you're willing, but in her heart she knew her own weakness.

That's it, thought Jamie. The price. The bit they don't listen to. Like the small print on the HP agreement. And they all fall for it, and wake up weeks later wondering how they could have been such mugs.

"There's nothing wrong with sex," Graham said, shaking his head to emphasise the point. "It's not a sin. But the wrong use of sex is sin, and the use of sex outside of marriage the Bible says is a sin, not because God doesn't want you to have a good time, but because God wants to protect your future marriage. He wants to save you from psychological scars and terrible guilt."

Carol's mind was racing ahead all the time, trying to balance things she didn't understand but longed for against what she knew and clung to. "Your future marriage"—she supposed that really lay behind her refusing Jamie all the time. The biggest thing in the world for her (a minor conquest for him) should be saved up, like a Christmas present, for the right moment, not squandered behind the bushes in the park, or silently, not daring to cry for joy, in a bachelor bedroom.

"You see," the voice hammered away, the bright spot of light dazzling her eyes as she concentrated, multiplying into a vast white sun obscuring the surroundings, hurting, aching, throbbing like a great agony, "you see, the human soul is so large that the world cannot fill it. All the popularity and money and sex cannot fill your soul. Only God can fill it.

"I'm going to ask you to do something difficult tonight," said Graham, dropping his voice almost to conversational level again. 'I'm going to ask you to get up out of your seat, hundreds of you, and come and stand reverently in front of this platform, and say by coming, 'I want Christ in my heart, and I'm willing to receive him . . . I want my sins forgiven, and I'm ready to change my way of living."

Jamie leant forward to see if anyone was going to be mug enough to move. The whole arena was silent and tense. For one joyous moment he thought nobody was going to budge. But then a young coloured bloke near the front stood up, and suddenly there were people coming from all directions (the ones with badges, too—decoys, most probably) and filling the space in front of the platform.

Carol watched them, too, envying them the swift response, the clean, quick decision. To her, the issue was simple, but hard to resolve. Either her life was Jamie's, for him to trample on, or use, or ignore; or it was God's like Aunt Sarah's. Jamie might, she supposed, fit into the second (though the mind boggled); but God would not fit into the first, she was sure of that. It was a straight choice. She leant forward in her seat, tense. If she could stand up, and go forward like the others, perhaps the issue would be settled. It was only a gesture, she realised that, but it would be something clear-cut. With a mental effort that made her gasp she stood up. Almost before she knew it she was walking down the steps, joining the crowd pressing towards the front; and the weight on her mind had lifted, the light had stopped hurting her eyes. Almost unseeing, she moved forward, with a sudden lightness she could not have believed possible, wanting to cry, but with relief, not sorrow.

Jamie spotted her as she joined the crowd at the front. It wasn't possible, he told himself, not her. Swallowed the lot? How could she? The evening went sour on him. It was bad enough her being so high-minded about bed, but to have her Bible-bashing as well would be the end. He'd have to sort her out quickly, before some of these Grahamites got their hands on her.

"Wonderful, isn't it?" the parson next to him enthused suddenly, face alight with the rare flush of success. "All those hundreds of sheep gathered in!"

"Sheep's about the right word," Jamie almost snarled as he rose from his seat. "How stupid can people be?" As he stalked off the clergyman was still gazing after him, jaw loose, eyes wide, the flush of success now the rose red of out-raged horror.

Jamie pushed his way through the crowds towards the exit. One group were singing hymns, another crowd were gather-ing around a tall parson who was holding a placard on a pole. "ALL SAINTS BARKING", it said, which forced a grin to Jamie's face. Not one yap among them, he thought, but quite a few pussies, I expect. He also saw a notice outside a booth labelled STEWARDS, which said, "WALK WISELY TOWARD THEM THAT ARE WITHOUT". Without what? he wondered, and decided it was probably without tickets.

What a ruined, wasted, futile evening it had been. He kicked viciously at a screwed up newspaper. Carol falling for this religious line just about capped it all. He should never have let her talk him into coming in the first place. On principle, he hated wasting a whole evening, but the talent here was not up to much, or inaccessible, and there was nothing else to make it worth while. Even the bars were closed.

It was at that precise moment that Jamie saw Denis Lancaster coming out of a room labelled Press. It was worth a try, and at best it might salvage a little gain out of this disastrous evening. He bore down on the unsuspecting show critic of the *News*.

"Good of you to come tonight, Mr Lancaster," he said, offering his hand and smiling warmly. "Hopkins, Jamie Hopkins."

Lancaster watched him warily, mumbling something that could have been "Pleased to meet you."

"I'm sure Mr Graham—Billy—would want me to thank you for being with us tonight."

"You know Graham?" Lancaster clearly wanted to be off, but professional instinct made it impossible for him to reject a possible story without testing it for size.

Jamie smiled in a self deprecating way.

"It's a privilege, being a friend of his." Sincerity sparkled from his eyes.

Lancaster settled into the routine, still testing.

"Is he tense before the meeting. Graham I mean?"

"Well, it's not exactly a pint, a sandwich and straight on," Jamie said, watching his accent, still smiling.

"Are you a parson, then?"

Jamie shook his head. "No. Showbiz. Perhaps you saw me on the platform."

"Why should someone in show business be on Billy Graham's platform? What is his interest in you?"

"My religious convictions," Jamie replied, eyes still brightly sincere. "You see, people from all walks of life lend their presence . . . sort of moral support. Scientists, politicians, athletes. I was flattered to be asked to represent the showbiz world at tonight's meeting."

"Hopkins, was it?" Jamie nodded. "Do you have an engagement at the moment?"

"Oh yes," he lied cheerfully, "regular." Suddenly the born liar's instinct warned him of dangers ahead. "But for contractual reasons," he added hastily, "I must not mention where. It's a . . . private club." Having thus dignified the Drum, Jamie decided to call it a day.

"Mr Lancaster, I must make one thing clear. I wouldn't like to use a wonderful occasion like this to further my career. You will appreciate that what I've been saying is not for publication. I'm really here just as an ordinary person supporting somebody I truly admire."

Lancaster surveyed him closely, tolerably sure it was counterfeit, but not sure enough to be downright rude.

"Fair enough," he said, ending the interview. "Best of luck, Hopkins."

Mrs Burry drained the last dregs of her gin and It. The room was hot and noisy. You used to get a better sort of clientele in here in the old days, show people, dancers, young officers from Chelsea barracks; but now it was mostly blacks, not drinking much but kicking up a din, laughing and singing and getting cheeky near closing time. Still, it was warm, and it suited her. Nobody really knew her here, that was what she liked about it. She could sit and think, and have a drink or two, and talk to some of the young lads (even some of the young darkies were quite nice), without her neighbours and other nosy people looking and pointing and dropping insinuations.

Take tonight. She'd got here about eight, after finishing off the bottle of sherry Carol's young man had turned his nose up at, and had had three or four drinks, and done some really hard thinking. Now she'd made up her mind, she felt better.

The way she saw it, her upstairs room was being wasted. For one thing, little Miss Turner didn't appreciate it. For another, she didn't much like having another woman around the house. For another, she couldn't stand that insufferable young man what-was-his-name . . . Jamie. (Stupid name, wouldn't have got away with that one in the Forces.) And for another, there were plenty of lonely young men living in bed-sitters who would jump at the chance of a nice little place like that. The rent would be very reasonable, but she would expect them to be friendly. If there was one thing she couldn't stand, it was people who gave themselves airs, or thought they were too good to mix with ordinary folk. No, she'd made up her mind. Carol Turner would have to go, just as soon as she could find a suitable young man. A card in the newsagent's window ought to do that.

She got to her feet and made for the door, a bit fuzzy in the head, but happy; it was nice to get things sorted out in your mind. Carol would go, and good riddance; and a nice, friendly young man would come. That sounded like a satisfactory swap.

Carol turned into Cromwell Road, feeling almost dizzy with excitement, but happy. It was nice to get things sorted out in your mind.

"It's like finding the key to a jigsaw puzzle . . . It's finding the key of your life." Sunset behind her, street lights flaring into life, the traffic and people pushing past, and inside her . . . what was it? Contentment. Understanding. Peace. That was it, peace, like the quiet after a battle or the calm after the storm has blown itself out. She grinned into a shop window. Aunt Sarah would be surprised. Her harmonium had done the trick after all. Or her prayers, perhaps. For a moment she caught a fleeting vision of Aunt Sarah, big print Bible open on the bed-spread, kneeling by her old, high bed with the brass knobs on, head in hands, carpet slippers half off her feet, telling God about Carol and asking Him not to let her get lost in the wicked city. She must tell Aunt Sarah as soon as possible.

Jamie jumped up on the low music dais.

"Go on," Mary said. "If you've been to hear Billy Graham, show us what he's like."

" 'E never will, will 'e?" one of the regulars squeaked. "I mean, what's 'e know about Billy Graham?"

"Shut up, all of you. I said I'd tell you, didn't I?"

A respectful, expectant silence descended, most unusual at The Drum. Jamie, furious at Carol but mildly elated by his skirmish with Denis Lancaster, badly needed some applause, and knew how to get it.

"Ladies and gen'lemen," he said, almost catching Graham's Southern vowels. "I'm here to tell you that you've got to give up every one of those wicked sins—the immorality, the lyin' and cheatin' and lustin'. All of it's gotta go. The Bible says it's gotta go."

"You'd have time on your hands, Jamie," shrieked a woman's voice, and the public bar erupted into helpless mirth.

Jamie smiled, pleased, well in control, the cameras in position and red lights on. He picked up a tray off the piano.

"He carried his big Bible like a waiter with a tray," he said, balancing it on his finger-tips. "But what a menu. The Seven Deadly Sins for breakfast, Salvation and chips for dinner, and Heavenly Glory for tea." Again, the laughter. Jamie waited. "Kindly pass the Alka-seltzer," he added at last, to set it all going for the third time.

Carol closed the bedroom door. She was glad Mrs Burry was still out. She didn't want anyone or anything to break this wonderful feeling of contentment. She felt she knew herself, in a way she had never done before; not as a secondary being, dependent on someone else (her mother long ago, Aunt Sarah, Jamie), but as a person in her own right. She felt made new, complete and whole. She didn't know much about God, she realised, but she knew He was there, real; more real, at this moment, even than Jamie, whose high place He had taken.

There was a rattle at the window, and then a low whistle. Carol's stomach turned over.

"Oh God," she whispered, standing quite still in the darkness of the room. The test was coming sooner than she had expected. Couldn't He have given her a bit of time to get to know Him, before this encounter she was dreading?

Of course, she could put it off. If she kept quiet, Jamie would go away. There were no lights on. For all he knew, she hadn't come home yet. Her heart raced and her palms pushed against the wall behind her. If he went away, she might never see him again, and it would be her fault, her decision. More time, that's what she needed, time to think.

For a moment she stood there motionless, but when she heard Jamie's footsteps going away, sheer panic drove her to sudden action. She flew across the room and flung the window open.

"Jamie!"

He stopped and turned.

"I thought you were out. Where have you been?"

"I missed you. At Earls Court."

"Come on down and open the door. I've got some good news. Where's your watch dog, then?"

"She's still out."

"Good. Then throw the key down."

Carol hesitated. She could never remember feeling so confused. Oh God . . . How could You do it? She loved Jamie—there was nothing wrong in that, was there? So long as he wasn't an idol. Well, he wasn't, not any longer.

"Come on," Jamie pleaded, "the key."

"Not tonight, Jamie."

He detected the uncertainty in her voice.

"Got a memory like an elephant, you have. One little slip, and a bloke's doomed for life." He went down on one knee, in mock supplication. "Please, little bird?"

Carol weakened fatally.

"Just talk?"

"Just talk. Promise."

The key caught the light from the lamp at the mews entrance as it flew, like a thin silver line from one world to another, down to Jamie below.

Carol waited by the window as he made his way in and upstairs. Usually she would have gone across and kissed him, but tonight she was confused, unsure of what she ought to do, or how she would react to it. Jamie glanced at her across the room and shut the door behind him. He had expected problems, and reckoned that ten feet between them was less worrying than a locked door and a solid brick wall. In any case, more than anything else at the moment he simply wanted to tell her about Denis Lancaster. He hadn't wanted to waste it on the morons at The Drum, but he badly needed to tell somebody.

He sat on the end of the bed, hugged one foot across his knee, and broke the story quietly and carefully.

"I've just been with Denis Lancaster."

"So that's where you've been," said Carol, completely failing to record the correct reaction.

"You know," Jamie said patiently, "the Show critic on the *News*. He's got the ear of every producer and agent in town. One mention from him and you're in orbit."

He paused, scanning her face for the surprise and admiration that should have been there, but weren't.

"Don't you see? It means I'm on the inside now. Somebody who knows everybody, knows me. And we got on very well . . ."

Carol hadn't moved from the window, nor registered any discernible response. Unable to ignore it any longer, Jamie stood up and walked over to her.

"What's the matter with you tonight?"

"Nothing."

"Come on, out with it."

"I don't feel like talking, that's all."

Jamie grabbed her wrists and pulled her nearer.

"Suits me," he said, "talking here's a waste of time, anyway."

He tilted her face up and kissed her gently. She let him but then pulled back slightly. At that moment the front door slammed. Carol froze.

"Oh no . . . She's home."

"So what," Jamie whispered. "You know where she can go, don't you?"

He pulled her back into his arms and tried to kiss her again, but this time she turned her head away.

"No, please don't, Jamie. Leave me alone . . . please."

He let go of her suddenly, almost pushing her away from him, and she saw that his face was twisted with scorn and contempt.

"You think I didn't see you tonight, don't you," he hissed, "Making a fool of yourself in front of all those people? Well, I did. I did."

Carol's face went white.

"I don't want to talk about it. It belongs to me."

"Then that makes it mine, too, little bird. Because you belong to me."

Again he grabbed her wrists, to pull her to him, but no

63

longer gently. This was the same game as before, but harder, and both of them knew there was everything to play for. For one moment the issue hung in the balance.

Then suddenly Carol let out a half stifled cry, pushed past him and ran to the door. Jamie tried to grab her, but she stumbled out of his grasp and down the stairs. Mrs Burry looked up from her dressing table, squinting to see better, head still a bit dizzy.

"What the . . ." She stood up just as Jamie half ran, half fell down the stairs after Carol. "Here, you two, wait a minute . . ."

She got to the door in time to see Carol running across the mews, with Jamie in pursuit.

"Don't bother coming back," she shouted after them, but they didn't even look round. Carol was almost out into the road, and Jamie, trying to keep his dignity, half walking, half running, was about five yards behind.

"Where do you think you're going?" he asked, darting forward and grabbing her arm.

"Leave me alone, Jamie," she pleaded, almost sobbing, tears running down her face, "please leave me alone!" She shook off his grip and turned on her heel again, running blindly down the road. Jamie hesitated a moment. Chasing a girl who didn't appear to want his company came hard to him.

All the same, he followed, catching up with her as she stopped at a cross-roads.

"Who do you think you are?" he hissed into her ear. "Somebody's plaster saint?"

Carol looked at him pleadingly, but he just stood there, taller and stronger than she was, sweat on his face from running, and anger. It was time she wanted, time to think. God, couldn't You *do* something? As if in answer, she noticed over Jamie's shoulder that there was a church across the road. Almost unconsciously, as though drawn irresistibly, she dodged round him and started towards it.

"Now where are you going?" Jamie asked, but he got no answer. For a moment he again hesitated, and then set off after her.

"Oh"—seeing where she was heading—"a church. That's great! Perhaps you want to pray? Well, look . . ." he drew abreast of her, put his hand on her arm . . . "If you want to pray to anyone, pray to me. At least I'll answer you, even if it's only to knock some sense into that stupid head of yours."

Carol shook her head, eyes closed as though to keep out visions she could not resist.

"I won't listen to you, Jamie. Please leave me alone."

Then, suddenly, she broke into a run again and made the church steps, sanctuary, sacred ground. Once there, she paused, uncertain what to do next, then turned to face Jamie as he walked slowly across and stood a few feet away, grinning, but not with pleasure. For a moment he stood there, hot and untidy—it was getting warmer, close, almost thundery, the long build up to a storm on a July night.

"It's all make believe, you know," he said at last, quite softly, but taunting, provocative. "Just empty promises to line someone else's pockets."

He nodded towards the door.

"Were you thinking of going in?" he enquired. Carol didn't answer, but put out a hand and grabbed the heavy latch. "Go on," Jamie urged, "try it. Just see how good the promises are."

She put her weight on the latch, but it didn't move. A glance at Jamie—disbelief, panic—and she tried again. But nothing happened. The great wooden doors were shut, only an illusion of sanctuary, holy ground the other side.

Jamie was enjoying the scene now.

"You didn't expect to get in at this time of the night, did you?" Carol just looked at him, face tear-stained in the light from a street lamp, eyes large like a frightened animal cornered and helpless. Jamie took a pace nearer to her and she rattled the handle desperately.

"Look," he said, reasonable, persuasive, "they're afraid you might nick something, or muck up their nice polished floor. That door is locked to keep people like us out. They've got all sorts of good things in there that they're afraid of losing. Ornaments, candlesticks, gold and silver. Up against those, you don't think you count, do you?"

Carol let go of the latch, and looked up the road nervously.

"Want to try another one?" Jamie asked. "There's that big one by the park. Why not try it? Or any of them. They'll all be locked, you know."

Again there was a pause, silence, traffic distant but the night now heavy with heat and pressure. Suddenly something seemed to snap. Jamie's eyes blazed with anger. He stepped back and gazed up into the dark, stagnant sky.

"How about that, God?" he shouted, his voice echoing off the church walls. "No takers for a bet that one of your places will be open. How's that for a public image, God?"

Carol watched and heard him horror struck. She stared at the figure in front of her, arched in defiance, face twisted and sneering, and felt faint. She slid down to the floor, sitting on the top step, sobbing, face in hands.

"Oh God, help me," she muttered. But softly as she said it, Jamie heard.

"Get any answer?"

Carol's sob caught in her throat and came out as a noisy gulp.

"I want to know," Jamie said. "I really want to know. Because if you did get an answer, we'd be sure who was telling the truth, wouldn't we?"

Carol swallowed, trying to control her sobs.

"I can't explain it," she said at last, slowly but firmly, "And it might sound like nonsense to you, but I know I could get an answer. It's just that . . . I think I've forgotten how to talk to God."

Jamie looked at her, almost as though seeing her for the first time. She really believed it . . . that you could talk to God, only she'd forgotten how to. It was all so stupid, just like Carol, with her sparrows and her looking at him in public, not realising what those sort of looks really meant. It was funny, one of the funniest, craziest things he'd ever heard.

He began to laugh—real laughter, genuine, from some deep well of the ridiculous—and couldn't stop.

"That must be the funniest, stupidest, most tragic thing I ever heard."

But Carol looked up, baffled by Jamie's reaction, very small and helpless. She was pathetic, he decided. The time had come to try the other side. He moved beside her and put his arm round her shoulder, gently, protectively. As he helped Carol to her feet she tried again to explain herself.

"You see, maybe God isn't in there, anyway. Maybe he's out here, with us."

"Not with me, 'e isn't."

"I mean it, Jamie. Some day I'll be able to explain it to you."

Jamie gave her a reassuring hug.

"Don't waste your time trying to do that, luv. Come on, let me take you back home."

For a moment they stood on the church steps, very close, Jamie holding her firmly. With the tips of his fingers he tilted her face up.

"And no more of this running off on me, hey?"

Deliberately, as though obeying some stern inner command, Carol freed herself from his arm.

"Goodnight, Jamie," she said, softly, almost reluctantly, and she matched the words by walking away. Surprised by the gesture, Jamie watched her open mouthed.

"Look here," he shouted after her, "if anybody does any walking off, my girl, it'll be me."

But it wasn't. Carol didn't even look round, let alone stop. She bit her lip, afraid she might weaken.

"Don't bother to wait for me tomorrow," he shouted, a hint of desperation in his voice. "I won't be there."

Carol winced, but kept on walking. She saw the ruined church, empty and dead, life flowing past it, and only the sparrows there. When you were nineteen, and your parents were dead, and you worked in a dreary hole like Barry and Swallows, it was hope you wanted, and life ... a cheeky, restless young man meeting you in the lunch hours, everything in colour, all happening. It was all *that* she was walking out on, banking on a life (new life, new power, new dimension, he had said) promised by someone she had forgotten how to talk to. But she kept on walking, making a choice, dethroning one from his high place ...

Jamie watched her go. It shouldn't matter. There were plenty more where she came from, and she was no Miss World anyway. But he didn't like losing. And it hurt, more than he cared to admit.

It was all a bit spooky, too—this religious bit. He could understand her not wanting bed (not yet, wait for the wedding night—women's papers were full of it). He could understand if she wanted him to name the day, or give up gambling, or turn up when he said he would He could understand if she had raved a storm about his not calling for her on time that evening.

But this was weird. It was as though a God who didn't exist—who couldn't exist—had stepped between them, switched off his power over her and erected strange, shadowy barriers between them. She had never been like this before. It was as though she had become a different person. The old Carol (the real Carol) would never have had the nerve to walk out on him like that, to argue with him and shut her ears to his words, his promises and his threats.

Jamie looked angrily at the corner around which she had disappeared.

"She'll be back," he whispered to himself, but without complete conviction. As he said it, the threatened rain began to fall, big, heavy drops splashing the hot pavement, creating a clean, wet smell: it was nearly midnight, and distant thunder broke over the other side of the river. The hot spell was over, it seemed. Jamie turned up the collar of his jacket and strode off, rain running down his face, soaking his shoulders. It was the perfect end to the day.

5

Dr Berman's surgery was in a quiet turning off the Regents Park outer ring. It was a substantial Georgian house, with an imposingly weighty door and a solid brass plate: pulling rank, Jamie reckoned. He ducked behind his paper as the front door opened, but relaxed when he saw that it was only a patient. From his vantage point over the road he had now seen two middle-aged ladies leave the building, the postman bring the mid-day post and a laundry van call. It was warm again, the storm of the previous evening having given way to clear blue skies, to the well-publicised surprise of the citizenry. It was especially warm standing still in the open, and boring as well. At first he had run through a routine detective scene, but now he was fervently hoping that his mother would leave the house for her lunch break very soon.

He shifted his feet, the pavement being hot through the thin, if fashionable soles of his suedes. The door opened and Ruby Hopkins came out, walking off down the road in her genteel style, small steps (shoes killing her) and face set in what she imagined was a refined expression of boredom. As soon as she was out of sight, Jamie was across the road and inside Dr Berman's reception room. He looked around uncertainly. He had an appointment, in a sense, but the place was rather disconcertingly empty. He coughed. Nothing happened. Then he noticed a glass panelled door labelled 'Consulting Room', and knocked on it.

"Come in."

Jamie ran a hand across his hair, straightened his tie, and walked in, trying to look as servile as he could.

"I'm Jamie Hopkins," he said, holding out his hand. "Dr Berman? You remember, I phoned."

Berman was a large, affable looking man in his fifties, almost bald and wearing rather unfashionable rimless glasses. He was resting in a leather covered arm chair and eating a starch reduced health food lunch from a tray.

He motioned Jamie with his fork to sit down.

"Your time is valuable, Dr Berman," Jamie began, the phrases well rehearsed but convincingly sincere. "I'll come straight to the point."

Berman nodded affably and broke a piece of crispbread (with added vitamins).

"My mother would be livid if she knew what I was doing. She's very devoted to her work—I'm sure that's no surprise to you. In fact, I'd say it's her whole life. Why, when a friend suggests a special evening in the West End, time and again I've heard her say, 'Have to get my beauty sleep or things'll go wrong tomorrow at the office'. Mum's not one to take her responsibilities lightly."

As Jamie warmed to the part, almost believing it himself, Berman sensed that further moving tales of his receptionist's devotion to duty might erode still deeper into his lunch hour.

"I assure you, I'm quite aware of your mother's excellent capabilities, Mr Hopkins," he said, smiling patiently.

Jamie took this as the cue for the second act. He assumed an anxious expression, and spoke more softly.

"She's had more than her fair share of worry lately, seeing me through college, and all. We've got a great future planned, but sometimes I feel like chucking it in and getting any kind of job when I sometimes hear her sobbing in her bedroom late at night."

Berman looked up from his sliced apple and grated carrot. The last bit was a trifle melodramatic, but the boy seemed genuinely concerned about his mother.

"I can appreciate your concern," he said. "The temptation is always with us to settle for the short term goal."

Jamie sat forward in the easy chair.

"I'll be honest, doctor. I want desperately to keep up my college studies, but I can't bear what it's doing to my mum." He paused, and then added, very diffidently, "I was wondering, you don't happen to know of anyone who is in need of part-time help, do you? Would there be the slightest chance that I could do anything for you here? Clean up after hours, wash bottles, anything?"

Berman munched silently—food inadequately masticated being a major cause of peptic disorders—and scanned Jamie's face. The young man was watching him open-eyed with boyish sincerity, a hopeful smile masking a shade of doubt about his performance.

"All right, young man," he said at last, "I'll think about it. I can't promise anything, but I can always get a message to you, can't I?"

Jamie stood up, the interview over, being careful not to over-play the enthusiasm but wanting to sound appreciative.

"Thank you very much, doctor. I truly appreciate your sparing this time for me . . . in your lunch hour, too."

Berman waved his fork in a gesture of friendly dismissal.

"I expect we'll be in touch," he said.

"I took an opportunity to sus the doctor's place."

Fitch looked sharply at Jamie across the display of men's toiletries.

"I didn't ask you to do that."

Jamie ignored what he considered a stock response.

"There's some kind of alarm system," he said, deliberately vague. "I've got an idea, though."

"I'm not too comfortable with your ideas, Hopkins."

Again Jamie ignored the stock response.

"How would it be if I got a job in the doctor's surgery? You know, something part-time, in the evenings perhaps, when everybody's gone home. There's a possibility . . ."

Fitch tried hard to hide his bewilderment behind the standard mask of suavity.

"I'll have to give it some thought."

Jamie smiled sweetly at him, enjoying the effect he was creating, and turned to go. He paused at the shop door for an exit line he re-lived for the rest of the day.

"So will I, for that matter, Fitch," he said. "And I'll let you know what I decide."

As he made his way up into Piccadilly, Jamie was more excited than he could remember. Everything was working out just as he had planned. If Fitch thought he had forgotten that little business in the mews, then he was in for a shock. They despised him, he knew that, and thought he was just dirt, there to run errands and be thrown the odd pennies. Well, he would show them. To fix Hubert and Fitch and at the same time make a real packet himself—that sounded like a master stroke. And yet, soberly weighing up the situation, he was three quarters of the way to pulling it off.

To complete a really satisfactory day's work, he must now do something about Carol. He had been thinking about the night before, and had decided it was best forgotten. By now Carol would be bitterly regretting it and they could just pick things up as though it had all never happened. It was partly his fault anyway, for letting her loose at a Billy Graham meeting without him at hand to stop her doing something stupid. It was just like her—he grinned to himself—to do what the big man said. Very impressionable, Carol . . . and trusting. She probably believed it all, swallowed the lot. He should never have agreed to go in the first place.

Jamie glanced at his watch. Five-thirty. If he went straight to the mews he ought to catch Carol just after she got home from work. A bus slowed down conveniently in the traffic and he jumped on, darting up the stairs three at a time. The conductress was up near the front on the bottom deck, so with any luck she wouldn't get upstairs before Kensington High Street, which would be too late. Even eightpence was worth saving, when it cost you nothing but a spot of strategy.

Jamie knocked on the door of the mews cottage, and was surprised to find it opened almost instantly. Mrs Burry appeared, in full war paint, Forces sweetheart of 1944. She checked her enthusiasm when she saw who it was.

"Oh, it's you."

"Carol home yet?" Jamie asked, remembering the other night but playing it quite straight.

"No. She's gone." Mrs Burry began to shut the door, obviously anxious to get rid of him. "She doesn't live here any more."

It took Jamie a moment to grasp the full meaning of what she had said, but when he did he put his foot in the door to stop her closing it.

"She wouldn't leave without letting me know."

Mrs Burry looked over his shoulder up the mews, and opened the door again. Jamie turned and made way for a young man—nice, friendly, strong—who was pushing through to the doorstep. He smiled at Mrs Burry, who stood back to let him through.

"Straight upstairs," she said. "Make yourself at home." She gave Jamie a frozen grin. "See, she's gone. Hard luck, mate. Now, if you don't mind . . ." And he had the added mortification of getting the door slammed in his face.

Jamie stood in the middle of the mews, utterly baffled. It was like a bad dream. He even looked again at the mews cottage to make sure he hadn't called at the wrong address. In Britain—he knew the rules, with lots of his muckers in digs—you couldn't just throw people out on the streets. There was an Eviction of Tenants Act. You could appeal. There was the Citizen's Advice Bureau. Why, he had a mate at college who had sub-let two bed-spaces in a bug-hole near Notting Gate for six months, and defied the landlord, the police, the public health and the man from the rating office, just by knowing the book.

But if she hadn't been thrown out, why had she gone? And where? Still mystified, and suddenly and unexpectedly lonely, he made his way out into the main road and began the walk home.

Carol slammed the door of the key locker shut and removed the key. The strange warm wind that blows, in season and out, through London's underground system tore at her hair. She had no idea what to do or where to go, and could not ever remember feeling so utterly and completely lost. Jamie had said they were empty promises, and it began to look as if he was right.

Everything had gone wrong since that night at Earls Court. Everything. She'd lost Jamie. She'd lost her digs. She'd lost the simplicity of life as it was. And what had she got in exchange? Nothing. If this was God's idea of a "new life, with a new power", then He must have a weird sense of humour.

Mrs Burry chucking her out was the last straw. Carol

could have wept at the injustice of it. Half the girls at the store cheerfully used their digs to entertain their boy-friends. It was warmer and more comfortable than the back of a car, and you were less likely to catch a cold. Nobody threatened to evict them, not even Monica, who practically ran a call-girl system from her bed-sit in Paddington. Yet here she was, losing her boy-friend because she wouldn't go to bed with him, and her digs because the landlady thought she did.

And the way Mrs Burry went about it! Knowing there was no legal way to get her out in twenty-four hours, she had threatened to phone Barry and Swallows and tell them she was acting like a prostitute. Of course, old Johnson up in Personnel wouldn't mind—probably make a proposition himself; but he'd give her the sack if someone threatened to spread a story like that about an employee. ("After all, you know, royalty shop at this store. We didn't get that "By Appointment' sign by lowering our standards.") He would be sorry (so understanding, so free with his hands) but she would have to leave.

So that was her digs gone. Carol just couldn't be bothered to delve into the question as to why Mrs Burry should have done it. She never made any pretence of moral purity herself—there was obviously some other reason, but Carol was too tired, too weary, too lonely and lost, to fathom it out.

She stuck the key into her pocket and wandered out into the early evening. Seeing a church across the square, on an impulse she walked over and tried the door. To her surprise, it opened and she went in.

It was big inside, and dark, although it was not yet sunset by any means. It was cool, too, and as Carol slipped into a pew near the back and sat down she drew her cardigan up round her neck. Two candles burnt silently in the distant chancel and cast shifting shadows over the carved marble reredos.

She hadn't been inside a church since she lived with Aunt Sarah, and that must be at least eight years ago. And it wasn't empty and large and awesome, like this one. She had thought a lot about Aunt Sarah these last few days. Certainly now, without any digs, without Jamie, without any idea what to do next, she would normally have made straight for her. Aunt Sarah would have helped her—or anybody, for that matter. But she was rather old now, and in hospital, perhaps permanently. It wouldn't be fair to worry her with any more problems.

A verger came in through a side door—Carol noticed with surprise that he was coloured—and began to put out the candles, very slowly and meticulously, as though making the job last as long as possible. When they were extinguished to his satisfaction, he turned and came down the centre aisle, carrying the snuffer in his arms like a royal mace. When he saw Carol, he stopped and came over.

"I'm very sorry, miss," he said, in a soft, gentle voice, "but I'll be locking the doors in a minute."

Carol looked up at him.

"But it seems so early. I hoped . . ."

"Evensong is over. We lock up after evensong."

Carol picked up her purse and stood up. The verger suddenly noticed the tear stains on her face, and the look of distress in her eyes.

"You got a place to stay tonight?" he asked. "There's a Salvation Army hostel down the road . . ."

But before he could complete the sentence, she had stepped into the aisle and was running towards the door. She opened the latch noisily—it seemed to echo all round the building—swung open the heavy door, and made her way out into the street. Here at least there was life and movement, lights coming on everywhere, and people enjoying the warm evening after another hot, sticky day.

Carol set off aimlessly back towards the tube station. She supposed the sensible thing to do would be to go to the Salvation Army place—she didn't really fancy sleeping in the open air. But there was too much else on her mind for her to be able to decide things like that. A wave of self-pity swept over her. She hadn't done anything wrong, she had believed what Billy Graham had said, she had trusted God— and look at the result. With awful clarity she saw herself: five feet nothing, assistant at Barry and Swallows, blonde hair (straight and shoulder length), nineteen years old and utterly, utterly alone.

Fighting depression, she opened the locker at the station and took out a suitcase. She carried it into the ladies, where she slowly washed and then put on an extra sweater. She noticed the attendant in the mirror, watching her.

"What's the matter, luv? Got nowhere to go?"

The words were kind enough, but the expression was not, a twist to the smile, and too much eagerness in the eyes. Carol stuffed her comb in her pocket, stuck her cap on her head, picked up the case and got out as quickly as possible.

Outside she looked up and down the road. Something near to panic engulfed her. It was not being without a bed—there was at least a couple of quid in her purse. It was this overwhelming sensation of isolation, even though there were people everywhere. God and Jamie, she thought wildly, where are you? You took his place, now where are You? If You can't help me Yourself, then let Jamie come and help me.

God and Jamie, she thought, picking up the case again and setting off along the street, I belong to you both, and I don't really understand either of you. The pairing didn't seem incongruous: after all, they had fought for the high place in her heart and one of them had won. And they both played games with her, loving her and leaving her, and both were a million miles away tonight, when she wanted them most.

God and Jamie, she muttered, crossing the road, following a familiar route as though by force of habit, please, *please*. A man in a shop doorway laughed as she passed him, and she realised she had been talking aloud. She quickened her pace, the case tugging at her arm, her fingers almost numb; down the alley, lean on the corrugated iron, squeeze through the gap, and she was inside. For a moment it seemed very dark, and there were no birds, but she hoped —blindly, without any reason—until her eyes grew accustomed to the light, and she saw with a sick sinking of the stomach that the ruin was empty. There was nobody there, certainly not Jamie, and probably not God, either.

She walked through the grass and weeds to the stone where she sat in the lunch-hours and put down her case. It was not nearly so warm now, and she was glad of that extra sweater. Above the sky was darkening, and the gaunt walls seemed in the half light to be leaning inwards, black and menacing. Yet, in a way, she was happier here than out on the streets. This was 'their' place, hers and Jamie's . . . and, in a way, she supposed it was God's place, too. At night it seemed different. Without the noisy life flowing by just outside, without the people in the offices around, it was less like a place of death in a sea of life. Now all was quieter, and the churchyard quietest of all.

Perhaps she ought to try to pray. The lady who had talked to her after the Earls Court meeting had gone on a bit about praying, which was all very well, but what did you pray about? And how do you talk to God? She hadn't told her that, or if she had, Carol had missed it in the excitement.

Still, she used to pray, when she was at Aunt Sarah's. And at school they had said prayers, like the 'Our Father'. But could she remember it? Carol screwed up her eyes and put her face in her hands, more in search of the words than as an act of piety.

"Our Father," she whispered. A pause. "Which art in heaven." There she came to a halt. What came next? Her mind was a blank. She tried again. "Our Father which art in heaven . . ."

And suddenly it came to her, not the words of the prayer, but the most wonderful, incredible thought she had had for hours. It was so startling that she sat in silence working it out, grasping all its implications. She had been feeling so desperately alone all the evening, and yet she had just called somebody 'Father'—'Our *Father*', that's what it said. Now if God was her Father, she wasn't really alone at all, even if she felt she was. She clung to the idea like a limpet. This was what it was all about, she decided: knowing that God was there, and cared, and loved you, and was your Father.

"Our Father," she said again, out loud, just to enjoy the words. And then she said it again, but softer, and dared to make it even more personally hers: "My Father."

She opened her eyes, and the ruined church looked like home. She was staying here, she decided, at least for the night, here where she had friends and could wait for Jamie.

77

Nobody would disturb her, and there were warm clothes in the case. With feminine thoroughness, her spirits quite amazingly lifted, she began to sort through her things and prepare for a night under the open sky. Well God, she thought, You've done something for me. Now if You could just send Jamie along, that really would be a miracle. Seeing he hadn't the slightest idea where she was, or even that she had been thrown out of her digs, and that his last words to her were 'Don't bother to wait for me tomorrow, I won't be there', that would be asking a lot, even of God. But she was in the mood for miracles, and there was (in Mrs Burry's favourite phrase) no harm in hoping.

Jamie had nearly reached home, still utterly baffled by the disappearance of Carol. However much he kept telling himself it was no concern of his (hadn't she walked off on him twice the previous evening? And when had a bird last dared do that to him?), he couldn't get her out of his mind. Heaven knows he'd tried hard enough. Even the frequent recapitulation of his stunning exit line at Fitch's, or the contemplation of the expert way in which the Plan had been carried out thus far, failed to do the trick for more than a minute or two. What was the point of having a Plan, or of outwitting villains like Fitch or Jenkins, if there were no one to tell about it and enjoy the fruits of triumph with? It was no good telling himself that girls like Carol were two a penny. So what? There was only one of him, and she suited him nicely, fitted in with what he'd got planned. Even this religious stuff, which was the real cause of all the trouble, didn't change the fact that she was his girl until he decided to end it.

And he liked her: not in this new, bolshie mood, but the way she really was underneath, handy, neat, unquestioning. He was not just using her, or anything like that. In fact, she was probably the nicest girl he'd had. Not as dishy as Veronica, not as intelligent as Claire, not as sophisticated as (what was her name?) ... Darlene; but she suited him better than all of them.

Finding her would take some doing, though. He stopped, almost on his own doorstep, to work it out. Where would she be likely to go? She couldn't get digs at such short notice, and she didn't have any special friends at the store who would be likely to put her up. Poor kid, she was probably feeling pretty lonely and frightened, unless she was in a hostel or something.

It was no good. A needle in a haystack would be easy to find compared with this. The logical thing to do would be to go home and wait for her to get in touch with him, or call in at Barry and Swallows sometime tomorrow. For that matter, knowing Carol, she'd probably be waiting hopefully at the church tomorrow lunch-time as usual.

The church . . . now that was a thought. It was crazy, but it was the sort of thing she might just possibly do if she was upset. The place was private, not too far away, and it was 'theirs'. On an impulse, playing a hunch, not really expecting anything but unable to go to bed and forget about Carol and her troubles, he sprinted down to Cromwell Road, and jumped on a bus headed for the West End.

Carol was dozing off, her back aching because of the awkward position, but her mind less agitated than earlier. A sudden sound from the far side of the church woke her up. She sat up, startled. The corrugated iron creaked and squeaked, and through the gloom she was sure she could see a shadowy figure slip inside. She stood up, heart pounding, as someone pushed through the bushes, along the over-grown path only she and Jamie knew about.

"Jamie!"

The moment of recognition was so intense and over-whelming that the cry of recognition was almost a scream, and echoed deafeningly off the stone walls.

"Hey, go easy, little bird," Jamie whispered, hugging her and addressing her left ear, "we don't want the Flying Squad dropping in."

Carol was crying and laughing, burying her face in his shoulder.

"Oh thank you," she sobbed, "thank you. Thank you."

"Don't thank me," Jamie muttered modestly.

"I wasn't," she whispered, and meant it.

The next hour was like a dream for Carol. She was sure Jamie would think she had been struck dumb, but there are some things you can't put into words. All of a sudden she was happy and contented, quite satisfied to let tomorrow look after its own problems. God had not let her down, and neither had Jamie, and now she was so grateful to the one, and so glad just to be with the other, that she could have wished the moment might last for ever.

With a great deal of laughing and giggling, and light-hearted hugs and kisses and glances full of awareness, they made their way back to the tube station and got her case out of the locker. She wasn't sure what Jamie was doing, but he took charge of her just like a husband (she'd never dared even to think that before) and she followed along, trusting him and not wanting to mar the magic mood by asking questions.

They got on another bus, bumping the case upstairs and laughing so that people thought they were drunk. It must have been very late—almost the last bus—because when they got off it in Earls Court there was hardly anybody about and the night was very still, warm and quiet. By now she had realised that they were going to Jamie's house, and she wondered what he would tell his mother, and what he intended should happen.

Suddenly Jamie spoke, his spare arm catching her hand protectively and folding it under his arm.

"Couldn't have you wandering about London all night by yourself, could we?"

She felt she might be permitted one tiny question.

"Are we going to your house?"

Jamie nodded. "And there's nothing to worry about, if that's what you're thinking. My mum's better than six watch dogs."

Actually, that wasn't what she was worrying about. In fact, she wasn't very worried at all, at that moment, and just smiled at Jamie with what he called her embarrassing look.

"Anyway," he said confidentially, "we can talk about it all tomorrow. I've got a few other things to tell you, too."

They slowed down as they neared the house, both of them

80

feeling a bit reluctant to end the experience. Carol, of course, had often dreamt of this—Jamie strong and protective, gentle and yet firmly taking the lead. But for him it was new, this surprising feeling of contentment and well-being, just through her being there. He'd never thought of it before, but it occurred to him that you could never really be completely happy on your own.

Carol voiced her one minor fear.

"What will your mum think—I mean, she doesn't know I'm coming, does she?"

"Oh, don't worry about her. She won't mind," he said, fishing out his key and escorting Carol over the door-step.

"That you, Jamie?" Once again his mother was spot on cue, voice coming from her bedroom. "Where on earth have you been?" There was some bumping and banging, and then she appeared in the hall-way in her dressing-gown, slippers on her feet, hair pinned up and face looking drawn and old without make-up.

Suddenly she saw Carol, trying to make herself inconspicuous behind Jamie's back.

"Oh, hallo my dear," she added, in her more refined voice, but plainly baffled to see her there at this time of the morning. She looked at Jamie for an explanation, and he took her elbow and steered her into the kitchen, leaving Carol to wait in the hall while he squared things with his mother. As it happened, he left the door open, and Carol, standing guard over her suit-case, could easily follow the drift of the conversation being conducted in fierce whispers just a few yards away.

"Why did you have to bring her here, at this time of the night?" Ruby asked. "Were you reckoning on me being asleep, heh?"

"It's not like that at all," Jamie explained. "She didn't have anywhere to go . . . got thrown out of her digs. I mean, I couldn't leave her wandering round London all night, could I?"

"All right," Ruby replied, "but just for tonight."

She sailed out into the hall, donning a smile of motherly welcome and concern on the way.

"Oh you poor child," she said. "Of course you're welcome to stay here . . . tonight."

Over the Weetabix the next morning, before Carol had put in an appearance, Ruby wanted the details filled in. Jamie realised this was part of the price, and decided to play it absolutely straight.

"Whatever are her parents thinking of," his mother began, "letting a young girl like that loose in London."

"They're dead. She's on her own."

Ruby pondered this, and came at the subject from another angle.

"Can she afford to pay rent?"

"Course she can. She's got a good job—assistant at Barry and Swallows."

Ruby's eyes widened with interest.

"Can she get things wholesale? I need some new clothes."

"Ask her yourself. I expect so."

The smell of burning toast interrupted the cross-examination, but after the pieces had been rescued, scraped over the sink, and brought like corrugated carbon offerings to the table, Ruby remembered something else she wanted to ask Jamie about.

"Oh yes," she said. "Talking about jobs, you managed that very neatly, sneaking in to see Dr Berman like that."

"Surprised you, did I?"

"The job's a possibility. He discussed it with me, of course, and we thought you could be quite useful during the holiday period. It might be a bit boring, you know—counting pills and putting them in little bottles, that sort of thing."

Jamie found it quite hard not to grin openly, but he managed it. Term ended the next day (their dump not getting university size vacations, like the pasty faced young gentlemen down the Strand), so with any luck he should be in business before the week was out.

The Reverend Andrew Gregory peeped round the door of his vestry. As he suspected, the church was empty. Row upon row of pitch pine pews gazed blankly back at him, the thick parallel slabs of dust-filtered sunshine chopping them up into tiny segments of light and shade.

It was always the same with this lunch-hour communion service. The bishop insisted—for the office workers, he said, serving the people where they are—but it seemed to him rather pointless. Only once in three weeks had he had the three people required by canon law for a communion, and that was because it had been raining.

He strolled out into the chancel, and discovered, to his surprise, that there was somebody in church—a rather attractive young girl, sitting about half way back, her eyes shut . . . praying, perhaps, or more probably asleep. He made his way down to her.

"Excuse me," he said, and Carol opened her eyes with a start. "I'm afraid it seems we shall not have the required minimum number of people for Holy Communion."

Carol just looked at him. She hadn't expected to see him, and she hadn't the vaguest idea what he was talking about.

Gregory was rather put out by her blank stare.

"It's regrettable, I know," he added, "the rules. But if you'd care to come next . . ."

Carol stood up.

"It's all right"—she gathered something was wrong, there was always some reason why she couldn't just sit there—"I only came in to . . . That is, I work near here. Came in to think, I suppose."

She gathered her handbag and was about to make off, but Gregory suddenly got interested in this girl who had come into his church to think. He dropped his official voice, and grinned at her.

"I wish everyone came to think," he said, with some warmth. "Half my job's done then."

Carol hesitated. The official vicar didn't interest her: people with plummy accents and smooth reasons for being stuck up and remote. But just at that moment he looked different, friendly and eager to help. Perhaps he was someone she could talk to. It was certainly worth a try.

"Actually I haven't been to church since I left Aunt

Sarah's . . . my Sunday school days. I lived with her for two years." She looked at him and he was smiling, listening attentively. "Aunt Sarah was one of the saints," she added.

"And you?" he asked. "Did you manage it, too—being one of the saints, I mean?"

"Just for two years. Then I had to move." Carol said it lightly, but it wasn't as flippant as it sounded.

"But something brought you back?"

Carol thought about that one, and decided to come clean.

"I went to Earls Court the other evening, to hear Billy Graham. Somehow it all seemed very . . . real to me."

Gregory nodded.

"If Billy Graham spoke to some deep need within you, then he was God's messenger to you." Carol nodded, and he went on. "Perhaps you'll find you also need the help of the Church."

This produced a more immediate and warmer response from Carol than he had anticipated.

"Listen," she said, quite fiercely, "I've tried. I really have tried. I feel as if I've been battering at the doors of the Church for days. You're the first Church person I've really talked to."

Gregory was a little taken aback, but played for time.

"I can understand how you feel about that. Still, in all fairness, er . . . I don't know your name . . ."

"Carol."

"In all fairness, Carol, you didn't knock on this door. We wouldn't have let you get away." He nodded towards the sea of pine pews. "We need everybody we can get."

Carol smiled, sharing his sense of frustration, won over by the reverse psychology.

"Look," he said, "you ought to meet some of our young people. Many of them have been through the same experience that you're going through. Why not let me introduce you to them at one of our home meetings?"

"Oh, I don't know." It sounded all right, but Carol was reluctant to commit herself.

"Well now," said Gregory, walking beside her as they slowly made their way down the aisle towards the door, the street and the world of men, "surely an intelligent, enquiring person like yourself wouldn't decide about us without giving us a first-hand examination?"

She grinned at him, and he knew that he had won. By the time they had reached the church porch Carol was surprised to find she had agreed to be called for that very evening and taken to (of all things, and what would Jamie say) a church house meeting.

At almost exactly the same moment as Carol was edging her way nervously into the church, Jamie was edging his way confidently into the drugs business. It was so easy he still could hardly believe his luck.

Here he was, two o'clock in the afternoon, Dr Berman out visiting a private patient, his mother having a late lunch down the road in the Soup and Sandwich House, and all alone in a room stacked with books and bottles, with instructions to clean it up. Cleaning up was just what he intended doing, when he had got the hang of the merchandise.

He guessed that the important stuff, including the mind expanders Fitch wanted, was in the locked glass cabinet. He had inspected it already, and wouldn't dream of paying its manufacturer the compliment of using a key on it. Ten minutes with a knife should be enough.

There was a U.S. Drugs Index in the book-case, and Jamie decided his spare time would be better occupied finding out what he was looking for. Fitch had mentioned two particular drugs, and he'd got the names written down on a bit of paper somewhere, if he could find it. Look them up in the Index, borrow a few samples to convince Fitch he had access to the real thing, and then he would be all set for the big plan, to fix Hubert and his boss and make a real packet himself. He cleared a space on the sofa big enough to sit on, and gave his full attention to the job in hand.

"Mr Jenkins in?"

The lacquered blonde looked up, no flicker of recognition.

"Mr Jenkins. I want to speak to him. The name's Hopkins."

"I take bets, see," she said. "That's what he pays me to do. Not arrange auditions."

Jamie realised he shouldn't have tried to by-pass the formalities. Fortunately Jenkins himself appeared from his office. When he saw Jamie he walked over to the counter.

"What do you want, Hopkins?"

"A word with you. Business."

Jenkins jerked his head towards the office door and Jamie treated the girl to one of his most provocative grimaces as he waltzed round the counter. Once inside the office, he decided to grasp the initiative.

"I'm willing to let bygones be bygones," he said, studying his expression in the cracked mirror over the fireplace.

"Why have you come here?"

"I've got something I think you might be interested in." Jamie took an envelope out of his pocket and slowly, making the most of the scene, opened it and produced a small white tablet. He handed it to Jenkins, who looked at it and then at Jamie, reluctantly interested.

"TCC," Jamie said. "An hallucinogenic drug. New stuff. A trip to heaven, they tell me . . . or the other place."

Jenkins turned his eyes back to the tablet again.

"Come from Fitch?" he enquired.

Jamie shook his head.

"No. This time I'm doing business on my own . . . and I'm not expecting that piece of information to reach Fitch's ears."

Jenkins handed the tablet back to him, discretion evidently triumphing over greed.

"I only deal through Fitch, you know that."

"But this isn't his stuff," Jamie protested. "I'm not taking any business away from him, or using his money, either."

"Not the point," Jenkins said, watching Jamie just as meticulously replace the tablet in the envelope and the envelope in his pocket. "Known Fitch for years. I'm safe with him. You go through him, and we'll talk money."

Although Jamie had expected this, he was not going to give in that easily.

"Now is that fair?" he asked. "I take all the risks and Fitch takes most of the money. That's no way for honest men to do business, is it?" He tapped his pocket. "These start at twenty quid each from the supplier, and" (remembering a phrase of Fitch's) "on our market they're like diamonds."

Jenkins eyes narrowed as he thought this one through, chewing at his cigarette and concentrating his gaze on the far wall. It was not the first time he had been compelled to make this sort of decision. In this business, getting it right separated the men from the boys.

"No," he said at last, removing his cigarette and blowing stray pieces of tobacco off the tip of his tongue. "Too risky. If Fitch weren't around, I'd take the chance. But he is, see ... and I want to stay in business and out of hospital."

Jamie nodded, smiling in what he took to be a knowledgeable way as he walked past Jenkins and out through the main office. He knew Fitch was the problem and he had expected to be told so. That merely strengthened his determination to get Fitch out of the way. To pay off a debt, remove a hindrance to success and earn—he'd been working it out that afternoon—£400 without risk or even serious effort: that was the sort of break he had dreamed about for years. And his plan would do it, he had no doubts on that score.

He looked at his watch to check that there was time to make the other call he had reckoned to fit in that afternoon. He spotted a taxi at the traffic lights and hailed it. There was no point in day-dreaming about earning hundreds of quid if you went on living like a beggar. From now on he would be travelling first class.

"Jermyn Street. Fitch's," he told the driver, and then settled back in the capacious rear seat. Struck by a sudden thought, he fished in his pockets for money, and was relieved to find that there was a ten shilling note he'd forgotten about in his wallet. The gesture would have been ruined if he had got caught for bilking at the end of the trip.

Fitch (Jamie now privately called him the Mad Hatter of Mayfair) took Jamie straight through into his private room behind the shop. The treatment had improved, Jamie thought, from a week or two ago. He handed over the envelope and Fitch removed the pill.

"TCC," Jamie said. "Hallucinogenic. Exactly what you wanted. You can't buy that stuff in Boots."

Fitch turned it over in his palm.

"I'll get it analysed, of course."

"I assumed you would, Mr Fitch," Jamie said, with just the right amount of sarcasm.

"Will you be able to deliver in quantity?"

"You leave that end of it to me. There'll be no difficulty, if your price is right."

"If the stuff is genuine, and if you deliver it in quantity, it should pay your pocket-money for quite a little while, Hopkins," Fitch observed. "Of course, should you be trying one of your little pranks . . ."

For a moment the two attempted to outstare each other across the room, then Fitch ended the interview by rising and holding the door open for Jamie.

Every gesture, every word, every inflection of his stupid voice, Jamie decided, made even more precious the growingly clear vision of Fitch, with the faithful Hubert beside him, in the hands of the Drug Squad and facing a spell in Wormwood Scrubs. No toilet water, no fancy black cigarettes there. Closed doors for Fitch, opening ones for Hopkins. The plan was so good, so satisfying, he wondered he had never thought of it before.

6

It was all happening outside, on the news-stands, in the Summer crowds, on the tops of the buses just visible over the high walls.

BOAC TAKES YOU THERE AND BRINGS YOU
   BACK
ANADIN WORKS FASTER
Fly to sunny Israel
NOTHING WASHES WHITER

Visit Majorca for £40, wipe away those washday blues, let the Army make a man of you, fly to Israel and die. It was all happening in the flowing tide of life on either side of the place, but inside, white walls reflecting the sun, butterflies hovering over the weeds and bushes, there was nothing to give it order or purpose. Yet inside, too, Carol thought, looking at the place with new affection, things were happening, things she had never noticed before. This was no place of death, as she had imagined. It was in fact a focus of life, the rectangle of its walls making a sort of tank in which specimens of life in profusion struggled to be born, and lived, and died.

Nowadays she often listed them, and added more each time. There were the sparrows and the pigeons, the butterflies and gnats and the wasps that hung around the rubbish and old cans so obligingly thrown over the walls; there were at least two cats that haunted the precincts from time to time, snails underneath some of the big stones, and worms on wet days; and there were the bushes, the nettles, the grass, the dock leaves and the dandelions, flourishing all around, filling the air with their dank, fertile odour. How she had thought it a dead place she couldn't imagine, except that it was easy to ignore life, when there was so much of it around.

What fascinated her was the power of life to survive and

overcome anything that would stifle it. The floor beneath her feet was a good example. Centuries ago men had laid these huge flagstones, and built this great church, its walls and spires pointing up above the city buildings. It had stood for their achievement, dominating the world of men. And now the men who made it were all dead, like Samuel Sebastian Grey (his works following him), and the great building itself was a ruin. Yet up through the floor, so firm and heavy, the grass and weeds had pushed their way, some fantastic power of life urging them on, until they owned the whole place, filling its last corners, covering its aisles and carvings, carpeting its holy places.

Carol grinned to herself. It still surprised her, to find that she could sit here now and think about something other than Jamie. It was also surprising the things she found herself thinking about.

But today she had come to do some serious and necessary thinking, and she had exactly forty-five minutes to do it. Events had happened so quickly lately, and there were all sorts of things to be sorted out. She opened her packet of sandwiches, which caused a flurry of anticipation among the sparrows, and decided to sample one of Ruby Hopkins' cheese and pickle specials.

Now there was one of the things that needed sorting out. It was ten days since that night (that wonderful night) when she had met Jamie here and he had taken her home. His mother had been very kind, really, after that initial shock, and seemed quite happy for her to stay (£4.10s. a week, extra for laundry and mid-day sandwiches). If anybody had told her a month ago that she would be living in Jamie's house she would have dismissed it as a hopeless dream of bliss. Now, the thing a reality, she had her doubts.

Not about her feelings for Jamie, despite seeing his worst side at home. After all, she had never had any illusions about him, she knew him, knew all about him. She still loved him, and her love now was more soundly based on a better understanding of Jamie, and of herself.

The doubts were about her own position. She was nearer to Jamie now, living in his house, but since that night (that wonderful night) new and more subtle barriers had sprung up between them and in some ways she felt further away from him than ever. He was a strange contradiction in his treatment of her: at moments, more tender and . . . she sought for a word . . . respectful than ever before. It was as though he had suddenly found out she was a person, with feelings and a mind and opinions, who resented being manipulated like a puppet. But at other moments he was ruder and more aggressive than ever, going out of his way to pour scorn on her faith and (did he know it, she wondered?) fighting tooth and nail to regain his old high place in her life.

It had become worse since she had started meeting the people from St Peter's. It was almost as though he were jealous, though Carol found it hard to believe he felt strongly enough about her to make that possible. He poked fun at any of them he saw, and made sneering comments at the supper table, at breakfast and any other time when his mother was around and she couldn't really tell him what she thought.

This was a disappointment to her, but it couldn't outweigh the tremendous difference being with these young Christians had brought about. Mr Gregory—the vicar—was very thoughtful and wise, but it was this bunch of youngsters, mostly about her own age, who had done most to shatter her prejudices about the church. They were alive, even more alive than Jamie, because they were real people who were not afraid to take a hard look at themselves and face the facts. That was where she had always failed in the past. She had become a sort of carbon copy of herself, animated only by Jamie and incapable of independent life. Now that had changed.

She remembered the first time she met them all, in somebody's flat. Mr Gregory took her there, and the first person he introduced her to had a face that was vaguely familiar. Eyes, nose, teeth: she had seen them before, though whether together or on different people . . . And then she had got it, just as the other woman got her, too: the Late Luncher, whose name turned out to be Gladys Byrne.

Gladys had almost exploded with surprise, her face going

91

red and words jostling across her lips in a sort of verbal anagram.

"You . . . the tickets . . . did you? . . . I mean, Barry and Swallows . . . the hat, in the sale . . . Billy Graham?"

Carol hadn't known whether to explode or die laughing. In fact she rather thought she had kept on nodding, her mouth shut tightly to stop herself giggling, but glad because Gladys was glad and in her life there had probably not been many moments of triumph like this. They had gone into a corner and Carol had found herself telling Gladys everything—all about Jamie, and Mrs Burry, and the digs, and the locked church, and the prayer that was answered, and how she was staying at the Hopkins'. And about Aunt Sarah, to whom (no doubt about it now), give or take fifty years or so, Gladys bore a striking resemblance.

And Gladys, in her funny way, which suited Carol, had been a tremendous help to her. She had set her off on reading the Bible, meeting her some lunch-hours and discussing the difficult bits. She had even taken her to church once, which was just as well because Carol was lost after the opening hymn and needed to have somebody she knew standing by to reassure her. And she listened, especially about Jamie, and seemed to talk good sense in her muddled sort of way. To her surprise, Carol found she had a boy friend, but he was away at college training to be a missionary. They expected to go to South America one day, to work among backward tribal people.

Gladys was very good at cheering her up, too. She seemed to be able to see through what people said and did to what they really meant. This had helped tremendously, especially where Jamie was concerned. Gladys said that he was acting as he was because of what was going on inside him.

"I reckon," she had said one day over lunch, "I reckon he's a very worried young man. From what you say, he's been used to manipulating everyone—his mother, the people at college, and you, Carol—and suddenly it's beginning to go wrong. I mean, you've started to make your own decisions and follow a path he refuses even to look at, and he doesn't know whether to humour you, or bash you into submission. Not only that," she had added, screwing up one side of her face to emphasise the tentative nature of her findings, "but I think there may be a deeper reason why he's so dead set against Christianity. Either he's got a very bad conscience, or right down underneath everything he's worried it might all be true."

Carol hadn't contradicted her, but it sounded highly improbable to her. But then Gladys had never met Jamie and had to rely on what she told her about him. Try as hard as she could, screw up her faith (as a grain of mustard seed), she could not visualise Jamie among the saints. The Bible said "all things were possible with God", but frankly she reckoned casting a mountain into the sea would be easy compared with getting Jamie on to the straight and narrow.

She rummaged in the bag for another cheese and pickle sandwich. She always ate those first, because she didn't like giving them to the birds. If what they did inside her by mid-afternoon was anything to go by, no sparrow could hope to survive their explosive qualities.

Her thinking time was nearly gone, and as usual she had reached no conclusions at all. There didn't seem to be any good reason why she should leave the Hopkins' house, and not even Gladys could interpret Jamie's present attitude with any certainty. Frankly, Carol was surprised he bothered about her, seeing all the trouble and annoyance she apparently caused him. She glanced at her watch. There was just time to re-read that bit she had read in the Bible this morning. If it didn't make sense after that, she would have to ask Gladys tonight. She found her Bible in her handbag, extracted it—quite a feat with a cheese and pickle sandwich in the other hand—and tried to find the place. A shadow fell over the page.

"What do you expect to get out of all that stuff?"

She looked up. Jamie was standing just behind her, bending forward slightly, an expression of eagerness to learn upon his face.

"Meaning to my life." It was brief, but it was the best she could manage off the cuff.

Jamie walked round and faced her, hands in pockets, playing the dominant male part he had understudied for years.

"You've got me," he said. "That's meaning enough for anyone." Carol smiled, simply because she couldn't help it. "And wipe that grin off your face," he added, but not unpleasantly, "because I mean it."

Carol took another bite of the cheese and pickle (she'd have stuck to salmon and cucumber if she'd thought he was coming) and looked up at him cheerfully.

"I can't help grinning. I'm happy."

"What have you got to make you happy, little bird?"

"Jesus Christ. He makes all the difference."

"You're getting embarrassing," Jamie said, pulling a face. "Talk like that is weird, cranky."

"I used to feel like that. But it's surprising how completely . . . unembarrassing it all is. It's as natural as breathing, and, well, so *real*, Jamie. That's the amzing thing."

"You're beginning to sound like an authority on God, you know. You'd better watch that."

Carol went on, however, as though he had never spoken, a train of thought having been set in motion.

"I just can't get over how it's a part of living, the missing part . . . the bit that makes sense of all the rest. I don't know . . ."

But Jamie cut in, impatient now, almost angry.

"Well, I know I don't want to hear any more about it. What's more, I want you to forget all this religious nonsense, too."

He looked at her fiercely, waiting for a response. Carol, churning over again inside, but determined to control herself, slowly folded her sandwich bag and put all the bits, and her Bible, neatly into her bag. Then she stood up, brushed the crumbs off her skirt, and smiled as sweetly at him as she could.

"You don't own me any longer, Jamie," she said very quietly, and walked off, leaving him stuck for a smart reply, silent among the nettles and dock leaves.

Jamie shut the front door and his mother's voice, on cue as always, came from the front room.

"Jamie? You're late."

94

He wandered in, angry inside, and wanting to wound somebody who couldn't wound back.

"So what if I'm late. Where's Carol?"

"How should I know," Ruby replied with some spirit, Jamie having touched on a sore point. "She's in and out of the house as if I don't exist. Goes out when she likes. Comes in when she likes . . ."

"And pays four pound ten a week for the privilege," Jamie snapped, not to defend Carol but because it didn't do to waste a good scoring opportunity like that.

"What about me?" countered Ruby, making the best of a bad argument. "I have a life, too. You tend to forget that."

She shouldn't have done that, he thought, using that refined voice on me. Not when I'm in this mood.

"What's stopping you, then?" he almost shouted, letting his teeth show. "Nobody's holding you back. You can go anywhere you like, any time."

"And what would happen to you if I did, I'd like to know?" She was a bit taken aback by the sudden outburst, but stuck to the script tenaciously. Their rows always came round to the same basic arguments in the end. "Who would get your meals? Who would look after you? That's what I want to know."

"You're not about to let anyone else try now, are you luv?"

Ruby ignored that remark and suddenly began to be very busy with her hands, sorting and folding the laundry.

"Not that I expect everybody to say 'thank you very much' all the time. That would be too much to expect." She managed to inject just a hint of tears into her voice. "But I'm not just your housekeeper either."

Jamie knew he had won, so he could be magnanimous.

"Well, what shall we do then?" he asked, in mock seriousness. "Fight? Or shall I sweeten you up a bit? I'm open-minded about it."

"That's right." Ruby turned to the sink, almost symbolically, and refused to be so easily deflected, even though she knew he had outsmarted her as usual. "That's right. Make a joke of it. Think you can get round everything with a laugh, don't you?"

Jamie knew the next move, and timed it perfectly, stealing

up behind her and putting his arms round her. She looked round at him over her shoulder, visibly softening.

"One of these days, my lad," she observed, but it was a statement of reconciliation rather than threat, "one of these days . . ." She disengaged herself, and waved towards the table. "Sit down. There's a fish cake warming in the oven. I didn't feel like much myself, so I stopped off at Sainsbury's." She paused, as though weighing up whether to reveal the next item of information, and then casually—too casually—started wiping her hands on a tea towel.

"Bert called, quite unexpected, just before lunch." She watched Jamie carefully. "We went to this darling little Italian place."

Jamie made no attempt to disguise his reaction.

"Blimey, not him again. If ever I've seen a load of old tat . . ."

"And what's wrong with Bert?" Ruby refined her voice again, but stuck a bit at 'Bert', which didn't go with the accent. "Aren't I entitled to a little happiness? He's gentle . . . considerate. And doing well at his own business."

"He's a butcher." It was quite amazing how shameful an occupation Jamie made that sound. "You call that happiness? Couple of pints in the local and a bit of slap and tickle afterwards. Happiness! The thought of him mauling you about makes me feel sick."

Ruby continued to wipe her hands methodically, surprisingly defensive rather than angry.

"Who are you to say he's like that. He's quite . . . respectful. You never know"—concentrating very hard on the wiping—"perhaps one day I'll marry him."

"Marry him!" Suddenly the game had taken a new turn, and Jamie hastily assembled his resources to cope with a new threat. This was the last straw—Carol turning awkward, and now his mother. It was really getting quite hard to rely on anybody. "Marry Bert? How could I hold up my head if you married that old twit? You can't mean it. Can you imagine how I could run a classy boutique if everyone knew my mum had married a butcher? It's not possible."

Ruby put down the towel, having got the reaction she expected and had played for. Now it was a draw, and she was content to play for time.

"I didn't mean it would actually happen . . . tomorrow."

"You deserve better," Jamie said, relieved that the threat was more tactical than real. "I mean, you're a cut above him, Mum."

Ruby sat down at the table, the dust of battle cleared, and Jamie's thoughts switched elsewhere.

"Did Carol say when she'd be back?"

Ruby shook her head.

"It was a meeting of some sort, I think."

You bet it was, Jamie thought, reaching for his jacket off the peg behind the door. It always is nowadays. She's got religious mania. It's properly spoiled her, though why that should bother him so much he couldn't quite work out.

"Going out?" Ruby asked, innocently.

"No," he retorted, because he felt like it. "I always put my coat on when I go to the loo."

He slammed the door behind him, and felt better when he found that two young girls waiting at the bus stop just by his house looked round at the noise, and then looked round again after making some comment to each other about him. He grinned at them (the taller one wasn't bad, actually) and for the first time that day the cameras moved into position and began rolling.

He decided to give the Drum a miss and try the more sophisticated bar on the corner by the tube station. It was almost deserted, being early evening for the sort of clientele they got. He thought about what he should order, and settled for a lager. There was no point in making an impression on the two loud-voiced salesmen at the bar or the elderly duchess quietly drowning herself in gin over by the imitation Tudor fireplace.

He'd got some thinking to do. The Plan could take care of itself, he reckoned, but it would need careful playing. A delivery of drugs was due on Friday—he had heard Berman placing the order on the phone—so possibly Friday night would be a good one. It was a pity, of course, that Friday night was a busy night for the fuzz, because they had an important part in the scheme of things. But he didn't expect them to let him down. He'd probably write to the Superintendent of Police, or the Home Secretary, if they did.

Carol was the worst problem, really. Four times now he had decided that she was more trouble than she was worth, and made up his mind to chuck her. Four times he had weakened. The whole situation was very tricky, because since that night (that wonderful night) there had been some new element in their relationship, some new, strong bond that seemed to tie them together even when they wanted to get apart. It was crazy, but with all her stupid new ideas—God, the Bible, praying, church and that stuff—there was also something new about her that made her much more interesting, more real—more desirable, too.

If only he could have Carol the way she was now, but without the religion bit: that would be really something. It should be possible. After all, the Christianity stuff must be bogus. Nobody believed all that spiel about angels and miracles and so on these days. So, sooner or later, if he kept on at her, she was going to have to admit it was all a fraud. Then everything would be all right between them. She'd drop those Victorian inhibitions about sex, stop seeing these stupid Christians she was spending so much time with, and in reaction she'd probably practically drag him into bed with her, out of sheer relief. He looked at the derelict bubbles at the bottom of his deep glass and pledged himself to bring about that highly desirable state of affairs.

Two hours (and two browns, one whisky and two martinis) later—the last three paid for by a revolting young man in skin tight leopard skin trousers, who seemed to be trying to get him tight—Jamie set off for home. He was not drunk, by any means, but he was light-headed and feeling quite pleased with himself.

It happened as he was passing the entrance to some lock-up garages. He heard a sound—half whimper, half groan—from the pool of darkness just behind the yard doors, which were open. He stopped, and heard it again. Normally he would have gone on, but the alcohol had made him braver than usual, and less cautious.

He stepped a few feet into the yard, and peered into the shadows behind the gate. At first he could see nothing, but then he heard the sound again, and something moved. For a moment he thought a huge dog, or even, crazily enough, a small bear, was hiding there, but then he saw that it was a person in a large, furry coat. Quite suddenly the figure lurched out into the light from the street, and stood in front of him, swaying and moaning. Then, without any warning, it collapsed again, but this time at his feet.

Jamie bent down, and saw that inside the coat, which was matted with dirt—and quite unnecessary on this warm evening—was a man, about thirty, Jamie reckoned, going bald, very thin faced.

"You all right, mate?" he asked.

Instead of replying, the man half rolled on to his side, so that the light shone in his face and lit up the top half of his body. Jamie let out an involuntary grunt of disgust as he saw for the first time that the man's left sleeve, and most of that side of his coat, was soaked in bright red arterial blood.

"What the hell have you done to yourself?" he asked. "Look, I'm going to get an ambulance." He stood up. "Wait there," he added, quite unnecessarily.

Jamie stumbled out of the yard and back down the road to the bar.

"Get an ambulance, quick," he shouted to the barmaid, "up the corner by the chemist's. A bloke's bleeding to death in the yard by the garages."

Out into the cold air he ran, head clearing with the effort, back to the corner. As he got near a sudden, awful scream came from the yard. He stopped, heart pounding, and then went towards the shadows again. Something was twisting as if in agony, gasping, sobbing, tearing at the ground. Jamie watched horror-struck, utterly unable to move or intervene, while the man went through his weird private ritual of pain, the movements jerky and hideous in the half-light.

It seemed an age, but it was probably three or four minutes before Jamie heard the siren of the ambulance, getting nearer and nearer, and people stopping at the entrance to the yard to stand and watch—as he was, but further back, not involved, just looking. The ambulance drew up and one of the attendants jumped out and pushed his way through the little knot of spectators. He stooped down over the man, and then stood up.

"Jack," he shouted to the driver, who was just getting out of the ambulance, "it's Mad Mick again. Bring the tourniquet."

Jamie watched as they took control, used to disaster, pain, blood and ugliness. They applied the tourniquet, bandaged his left wrist, forced something between his lips, and then lifted him on to a stretcher. After they had put him into the ambulance they came back to Jamie.

"You find him, son?"

Jamie nodded.

"Know him? Were you with him?"

"No. Never seen him before."

The driver looked at him closely for a moment, but said nothing.

"Why?" Jamie asked. "What's the matter with him?"

"Heroin," replied the driver, still watching Jamie. "He's a junkie . . . bad case. Third time he's been picked up this week. He's only twenty. The stuff's killing him, but he can't stop. They never can."

Jamie said nothing, too busy with his thoughts, and the sight of the blood and the horrible movements in the half-light.

"Sure you're not one of his friends?" the other ambulance man asked him. "You don't use the stuff, do you?"

Jamie shook his head.

"It's the people who sell it to them who ought to do our job," the driver said. "Scum of the earth. I mean, who'd sleep at night knowing they'd got rich doing that to people?"

Jamie heard, and saw, and thought of Fitch and Hubert and Jenkins . . . and himself, he realised, with a cold shiver.

"I've gotta be off," he muttered, and turned on his heel to leave them, the spectators parting to let him through.

Jamie flung himself on to his bed, not even taking his shoes off, and buried his face in the pillow to shut out the sights and sounds of the last half hour. Whatever he did he saw the ridiculous fur coat heaving and jerking in the shadows, and heard the sobs and that awful scream, and the siren wailing. He rolled over on to his back, and with his left hand flicked on the radio beside his bed, filling the room with pirate music. For a moment the sound held sway, and he found that by fixing his eyes on the crack in the ceiling and tracing it across to the window surround he could shut out the visual images. But only for a moment.

Insistently they returned, the thoughts insidious and un-nerving, the blood on the sleeve, the people who shouldn't sleep at night but do and the young man his own age who looked thirty and was killing himself. For some reason Carol intruded, too, a sort of total contrast, clean and bright and open, talking about God and forgiveness and all that stuff. He shut his eyes, which made it worse.

I'm not responsible for Mad Mick, he told himself, facing the spectre head on. If I didn't deal in the stuff somebody else would. If he's daft enough to take it, that's his funeral ... his look out. Anyway, he wasn't a pusher. He was just a sort of messenger boy, but about to get promotion into the supply side of things.

The radio was loud enough already, but suddenly Jamie leant over and turned the volume up to maximum. The whole room vibrated with the noise, his ears literally hurt with it, a great pent-up explosion of sound reverberating around the four plain walls beneath the ceiling with the tortuous crack in it. He held his breath, letting the noise drive out every rival for his attention, immersed in it totally. The vision and the voices faded, Carol, Mad Mick, the blood and the fur coat and the movements in the half-light, and he was himself again, getting rich and able to sleep at night.

Carol admired Jamie over the top of her soup spoon.

"Jamie," she said, barely controlling a giggle, "I don't know how you did it. I was petrified ... you could have lost me my job!"

"Go on," he teased, enjoying the underlying compliment, knowing which way to take it. "Saved you your rotten job, more likely."

For the second time (but Jamie felt it bore repetition) Carol recapitulated his recent triumphant performance in the millinery department. He had to admit, he'd been quite pleased with it himself. Rescuing Carol from an over-bearing, overweight lady of middle years and county accent, he had assumed the role of departmental manager and sold her for five guineas a hat for which even Barry and Swallows asked only two, solely on the hint that it had been specially created for Princess Grace and should never have been shown to the general public.

At the time Carol had been horrified, and for a few moments afterwards she had been rather worried that it was all slightly dishonest, but the incident ending so happily and the thought that her employers were the only people to make anything out of it kept her conscience quiet, at least temporarily.

As they laughed together over their soup, and Carol re-minded herself that this was the very first time that Jamie had ever treated her to lunch, she decided to seize the moment to ask what was, for her, an important question.

"Jamie, I'm going to a special meeting tonight. It's for people who've got questions about Christianity. Will you come? Please?"

He sucked a spoonful of soup noisily.

"Little bird," he said at last, "I've got a question I'd like *you* to answer. I've been thinking. If Jesus Christ is full of all this power you're supposed to have tapped, then why does He let the Church pass Him off as a museum piece?"

He put down his spoon and broke off a piece of roll, stuff-ing it into his mouth, waiting for the reply he knew wouldn't come.

"If I was Him," he added quietly, speaking with his mouth full, "I'd sue."

Carol, crushed, the magic moment gone, the lunch hour, like so many before it, ruined, had no reply.

She still had not thought of a reply by supper time, and the atmosphere at the table was slightly uncomfortable. Ruby could never understand what was going on. At one moment Carol and Jamie would be laughing together, whis-pering and giggling and teasing her. The next minute they'd be sitting like they were now, not exactly quarrelling, but silent, occupied with their own thoughts, and obviously not very pleased with each other. She'd given up trying to make ordinary conversation on these occasions.

It was Jamie who broke the silence, after watching Carol eating with unusual haste.

"Bolting it down tonight, aren't you?"

Carol chose to ignore the remark.

"Been having quite a time lately, haven't you?" he went on.

"Oh do stop it Jamie," Ruby said, sensing trouble. "Carol, how about a nice jam tart to finish up with, luv?"

"No thanks," said Carol, "I'm in a bit of a rush."

"Afraid God can't get on without you?" Jamie taunted. To his surprise Carol rose to it, eyes flashing.

"Look, Jamie, if you want to argue, I'll argue. But I don't see any sense in it."

This new-style display of spirit struck him momentarily dumb.

"Now, now, you two," Ruby intervened.

"Can I have another cup, Mum?" Jamie asked, playing for time. Then, trying a different approach altogether, "After all, Carol, I don't like you spending so much time at that . . . whatever you call it. How do I know what you do there? Or who you run off to meet?"

Ruby intervened again. "Well, it *is* some sort of religious meeting . . ."

"How many times have I asked you to come with me?" Carol butted in, throwing the question straight across the table at Jamie. "Didn't I ask you at lunch time?"

"Do you think I want to bore myself silly listening to a load of stupid Christians patting each other on the back?" Jamie knew it was weak, but he wasn't yet used to Carol in this aggressive mood.

"How do you know *what* we do?" she demanded.

"I know enough to know I don't like it."

This time Carol knew it was weak as well, and warmed to her theme.

"At least the people I meet there have open minds. At least they're trying to sort out what they believe. They're not

103

just burying their heads, afraid they might hear a bit of truth that would threaten them."

Ruby made a third, desperate attempt to bring the conversation back into charted waters.

"If it's church you're arguing about . . ." she tried.

"No, it isn't church, Mrs Hopkins."

"What else is it then, I'd like to know?" Jamie asked.

Carol stood up, and looked down at him from her five feet nothing.

"There's one sure way to find out . . . But you couldn't do that, could you? You wouldn't have anything to shout about then."

Carol started to move away towards the door. Jamie, not used to being defeated by her and not yet able to take it, tried his last, despairing move.

"I've got a smashing evening planned," he said, in his most persuasive manner.

Carol stopped and looked at him, almost pitying his utter inability to see what was really at stake.

"I'm not stopping you," she said, and later regretted it because it sounded rotten and bitter, and that was not how she felt for him. But the regrets didn't come until she was at the bus stop, which was too late to do anything about it right away.

"You should leave her alone, Jamie," Ruby Hopkins said, gathering up the dishes more flamboyantly than usual. "It isn't anything to do with you."

"I've got to protect the silly thing, haven't I?" he replied. "It thinks it's been saved, or some such rot. Someone's got to put it right again, haven't they?"

"All the same, I wish you wouldn't, Jamie. It isn't as if you're some uneducated savage who doesn't know right from wrong. You were brought up right, I saw to that."

"I know what's what," he countered, slightly amending her phraseology. "She's the one weak in the head, not me. I can look after myself, don't you worry."

He managed the exit quite well, slamming the door and jumping over the door steps. But it brought him little joy, because the choice before him out there in wild Earls Court was the Drum (Mary, the regulars, the whole stupid, noisy crowd) and the pub near the tube (high prices, nasal accents, French cigarettes and queers). He settled for the Drum, mainly on financial grounds, and began to tackle the task of raising his own spirits by his own unaided efforts before he got there.

Carol still couldn't believe it. Again she checked the people present, just to make sure she wasn't dreaming. At the far end, the vicar. On his left, Roger and Michael. Then, going round the room, Janine, Mary, Keith, Susan and Sandy. Bill and Anthea were sitting on the sofa (as usual) and on the stool was Gladys, looking . . . smug? No, triumphant, as though it was all her doing. And there, sitting on the arm of her chair, just between her and Gladys, was Jamie.

In all her life Carol had never been so surprised as she was five minutes before when the door had opened and Jamie walked in. Of course she was pleased, but shock and fear (fear of what he would do, what he would say) almost outweighed the pleasure. She looked at him, and he grinned, but it was not a straightforward grin and it left her worried. The only explanation he offered for his attendance was that after ten minutes at the Drum he got bored, looked up Gregory's name in the phone book, rang the vicarage and asked his wife where the house meeting was being held that night. That told her how he got there, but it didn't begin to explain why.

Gladys was rambling on in her own cheerfully disorganised way about prayer ("talking to God" was her usual definition) when it happened. Jamie, who had been watching everything with polite cynicism, suddenly unleashed a string of questions at her.

"Just exactly how do you hear his voice? God, I mean? Is it like ringing him up, when you feel like a chat?"

"Well, I suppose faith comes into it," Gladys countered, blushing, looking around the others for support.

Jamie's grin widened and got uglier.

"You mean you gotta have faith that there's Somebody listening?"

Carol tried to intervene on Gladys's behalf, but got no further than "No, Jamie . . ." when Keith chipped in.

"Gladys is right, really. It is a matter of faith—that God is there and Jesus Christ is alive. That's not theology, that's experience."

"Jesus Christ!" Weeks of pent-up frustration were spat out in the two words as Jamie turned on the unsuspecting young man. "Jesus Christ! Been dead for centuries, and you keep on about Him as if He were Harold Wilson."

There was an awkward silence for a moment, everybody stopping their conversations in mid-stream, most of them smiling to cover their embarrassment, but Carol wide-eyed with horror and shame, not able to move or speak. Everybody seemed relieved when Mr Gregory shifted in his seat and drew the fire.

"Dead for centuries?" he said, not aggressively, but leaning forward to give his question emphasis. "So you reckon He was just an ordinary man?"

Jamie grinned at him. "Yep."

"You really mean that?"

"Yeah. Mind you, He was clever with it. Made His name saying smart things . . . 'Turn the other cheek' and 'love your enemies'. That sort of thing."

"A good man?"

Jamie shrugged his shoulders non-commitally.

"One of the best men who ever lived, you might say?" Gregory pressed the point.

"*You* might. We never met," Jamie said, looking for laughs and a little put out that he didn't get any. As nobody else rushed to say anything, he added defensively: "Look, I'm sure He was a well-meaning bloke. But it's all such ancient history, isn't it?"

Gregory smiled, but took the point seriously.

"I should have thought the last thing He could have been was just a well-meaning bloke. He claimed to be the Son of God. There's just no dodging that. So if He wasn't the Son of God, that makes Him a lunatic or a fraud. Hardly qualifications for 'the best man who ever lived'."

"And if that's all there was to Him," Bill chipped in, "then the Sermon on the Mount was just a lot of double-talk to dazzle the crowd. He'd have been the arch operator of history."

Jamie opened his mouth to speak, but couldn't think of anything to say. Everybody was watching him, and for the first time since schooldays he was stuck for words. He looked at the vicar, not grinning now, but hoping that he would say something, change the subject and divert attention. Gregory thoughtfully obliged.

"That's always the crucial question, isn't it? Deciding about Jesus Christ . . ."

Jamie relaxed. That was quite nasty for a moment, finding himself up the creek without a paddle like that. He was a fool to have come, and a bigger fool to have tangled with this squadron of super-saints. It was all nonsense of course— everybody knew that—but some time he'd have to find the answer to that one about Christ being the Son of God.

It was not very comfortable sitting on the arm-rest, and if he got stuck here much longer he'd have a permanent rut across his seat. He leant towards Carol's ear.

"We've been here long enough," he whispered. "Coming?" She grabbed his arm firmly.

"No. And you're not going either," she hissed.

Jamie wriggled on the arm-rest and prepared for a long and numbing wait. But for the second time Gregory came to his rescue, offering him a leather cushion to sit on and a wall space to lean on. Not wanting to get caught again, Jamie kept quiet during the ensuing discussion, but he listened . . . at first to get ammunition with which to sink Carol, and later because, despite himself, he found the too-and-fro of argument interesting, and the people themselves unusually frank and honest. For the very first time—stealing a glance at Carol, animated, happy, drinking it in—he got an idea of what he was up against.

They took the long way home, by the river, through the little gardens flanking the tow-path above Chelsea. The evening was warm under a cloudless sky, the English Summer having so forgotten itself as to stay fine for week after surprising week, the pavements dusty and the grass unusually dry and scorched. Carol held Jamie's hand confidently and kept looking at him, as though she still couldn't believe it. Not since that night (that wonderful night) had they been so close, so obviously happy to be together. Never had she felt it all to be so right.

Neither spoke. Carol took Jamie's silence to be one of thoughtfulness—perhaps even the first, frail steps towards understanding and sharing her faith. He had come to the meeting, and while it was true he had behaved badly at first—she hadn't known where to look—by the end he seemed quieter and perhaps even impressed.

Jamie was silent because of thought, that was true. All sorts of conflicting ideas were chasing each other around his brain. The Plan, less than twenty-four hours away from execution; Fitch in the hands of the police and himself with his fingers in a very big till; a fur coat heaving and jerking, and bright red arterial blood; and Carol, too good to be true, leaning her head on his shoulder, almost choking herself with satisfaction, and asking . . . just asking . . . to be shown what it was all about.

He chose a private spot above the tow-path, well away from prying eyes, decently shaded and screened by bushes, and sat down. He held a hand out to Carol, and she sat down beside him. For a moment they sat and watched the river, its poisonous waters looking cool and pure in the moonlight, night turning evil to good, dulling judgement, warping conscience. Carol wriggled closer to him.

"It's so wonderful," she said softly, "really being together."

Jamie laid his finger on her lips for silence, but as soon as he withdrew it she went on.

"Jamie . . . You know, when you find out that God is real, and you can know Him, you feel that maybe the terrible loneliness we all know sometimes is really only the absence of Him."

"And who said that?" Jamie asked.

"I did," she replied, quite innocent of any sarcasm in his question. "I've been thinking a lot about it. I used to have terrible fits of loneliness."

"Not when you were with me."

"Mm. Sometimes."

He turned her face towards him.

"Turn it off, will you?" he said teasingly, kissing her gently on the mouth. "Don't you know when it's time to close that pretty little yap of yours?"

She looked hard at him, but in the darkness—judgement dulled, poisonous waters looking cool and pure—she saw only laughing eyes. She giggled and buried her face in his shoulder. He gently eased her down until she was lying on the grass looking up at him, embarrassing in public, but now the sort of look that asked to be shown what it was all about. He kissed her, much more fiercely, pinning her to the ground.

"But Jamie . . ." she gasped.

"Shut up," he said, not unkindly, but firmly. "I said I'd go with you, and I did. I didn't promise to believe it, and I don't. But I think you owe me something for the evening I've wasted on your precious church friends."

"Oh Jamie," Carol whispered, her voice catching with the utter disappointment of it, the disillusion. She struggled to get up, but he wouldn't let her, pinning her down again and kissing her so hard it hurt her lips. She tried to push him off, but failed.

"Just stop rabbiting," he panted, eyes not laughing now. "You're enough to make a bloke give up altogether."

"You're a fraud, Jamie Hopkins—a stupid, empty fraud," she said, lying still but uttering the words with biting clarity.

"I just want to love you, little bird," he whispered, trying that other tack, almost pleading.

"Love?" She almost sobbed out the word. "Love? All you know how to do is grab. Anything you want at the moment . . . just grab it."

"Well, what are you screaming about," he said. "I'm not asking much." He moved his hand to touch her breast, as though to underline the statement, and she took the opportunity to wriggle free. Pulling down her skirt, hair over her eyes, she knelt for a moment and looked at him, warding him off with her hands.

"Not much?" she said, gasping the words between clenched teeth. "You're dead right. Not nearly enough. That's the trouble, Jamie, you're not asking nearly enough."

He sat up, surprised at her outburst, taking a long while to learn.

"Sex," he said slowly and deliberately, as if giving a lesson to a small child, "is natural when two people are supposed to be in love. You're the weird one, Miss Dolly."

Carol stood up, tears running down her cheeks.

"It's not me you want! Anyone will do. Jamie . . . I want to share everything with you, my whole life. I've got so much to give and you're settling for a dirty little fumble in the dark."

Jamie squatted on his haunches, looking up at her in the darkness, angry, disgusted with himself for playing into her hands, hemmed in by unseen forces.

"Every time you open your mouth," he said cuttingly, it being the only thing left to say, "it sounds as if you're standing on a soap-box."

She had started to walk away, dishevelled, but with some dignity about her. Then she stopped and turned, as though considering the last remark.

"And you're so busy running and puffing yourself up," she shouted at him across the intervening five yards, "you can't hear anything except your own heavy breathing."

Jamie made no effort to chase after her or stop her. This was getting a habit now. But anger and petulance overcame him as he watched her disappear, and another emotion, too, which he wouldn't admit even to himself, because how could he hold up his head if he judged himself to be jealous of a God he didn't believe in, a rival who didn't even exist?

7

The day of the Plan dawned bright and warm. Jamie woke with a headache at nine-thirty, got dressed and shaved to ten-thirty and discovered that his mother had gone to work leaving only an empty Weetabix packet for breakfast. He looked for an egg to go to work on, but couldn't find one, and settled for bread and marmalade. He found the *Mirror* and flicked through it, but his mind was on weightier matters, such as his day's timetable.

Today being Friday he was due at Dr Berman's consulting rooms at two o'clock. He planned to arrive a little late, so that he could reasonably offer to work late to catch up. His mother couldn't hang around afterwards, because it was her night for Bert, his dart club not having a match, not wanting to waste good drinking time on pay-night. That also meant Ruby would get home late, possibly a little merry, and she probably wouldn't even notice that he wasn't in. Carol would, of course.

Carol. The trouble about having her in the house was that it made having a decent row very difficult. Normally he'd have kept her on tenterhooks for a week after an incident like last night's, but living in the same house it was almost impossible. Probably tomorrow, in the after-glow of the Plan, he'd take her out somewhere and they'd forget all about it.

She'd got this religion thing very badly. He realised now his mistake in underestimating it. He must be more patient, more subtle. Not for the first time recently he was mildly perturbed to find that he no longer even considered the possibility of dropping her altogether, and finding a girl who would present fewer problems, and not sell her miserable honour so dearly.

He had to admit, too, that all this talk about God was very disturbing. Once or twice recently, in unguarded moments, he had found himself almost uncannily conscious of some new element in his life, as though someone were trying to get through to him, almost pursuing him whichever way he turned. For a moment Jamie glared moodily at the paper (NURSES TRAP PEEPING TOM, said the headline), then he stood up and transferred his glare to the little mirror by the sink.

"If you want me, God," he said defiantly, "you'll have to get in line."

Dr Berman was just about to leave his surgery, having psychoanalysed all afternoon until he felt in need of therapy himself, when he noticed the light on in the dispensary. He opened the door and looked in.

"Oh, still working, Hopkins?"

"Yes, doctor," Jamie replied, his sleeves ostentatiously rolled up, dirty bottles all over the draining board. "I was a bit late in this afternoon, so I'm just catching up."

"Righto. Make sure you lock up when you leave. Goodnight."

Jamie grimaced after him as the door shut. He needn't worry. Those valuable pills and things would be safe as lollipops at a kids' party. He grinned to himself, and kept on cleaning bottles until he heard the front door slam shut.

Now that the time for the Plan had come he was almost drunk with the excitement of it. He walked over to the drugs cabinet, which Berman had so carefully locked not half an hour ago. With the aid of a sharp knife he had little difficulty in removing a pane of glass, and then he carefully selected the bottles he had previously noted from the Drugs Index. He wrapped them in brown paper and put them on one side.

Then he walked over to the phone, pulse racing, hands clammy. He dialled, and the phone at the other end rang three or four times.

"Mr Fitch? Hopkins here."

The answer was muffled but seemed to invite further conversation.

"You remember I said I could get you those drugs, the ones you wanted? Well, something's cropped up. The doctor's having a new alarm system fitted—the workmen have been in today dismantling the old one. It looks like tonight will be the night—tomorrow this place will be tighter than the Bank of England."

Fitch enquired what was preventing him from lifting the stuff on the spot if he knew so much about it.

"Well, as you know, I'm working in the surgery—a vacation job. Obviously I'd be suspect number one if anything was missing and I couldn't prove an alibi, wouldn't I?"

Fitch then asked rather icily the reason for this phone call.

"For a fifty-fifty cut I would loan you my key to the surgery," Jamie said quietly. "That's like holding the door open for you, isn't it?"

There was a moment's silence on the other end, and then Fitch suggested he should meet Hubert with the key at the post-box on the corner of Half Moon Street in half an hour's time.

"OK," Jamie agreed. "Make the job look professional. I'll see Hubert in half an hour. Tra."

He rang off and winked at himself in the glass-fronted cabinet. The die was cast. Fitch had all but held his wrists out for the handcuffs, and Jamie couldn't wait to hear them click shut.

He picked up the brown paper parcel, stuffed it in his jacket pocket, and went over to the phone again. Lifting it off the hook, he wrapped a handkerchief over the mouthpiece and dialled 999. He asked for the police and fidgeted with his feet while he waited to be put through.

"Police? I want to report a burglary. No, you can't have my name and address . . . just write down this address: 23, Cowper Gardens, W2. Got that? That's the scene of the crime . . . No, it hasn't happened yet, but it will—tonight."

He rang off, very pleased with the impression he felt he had created, and got out of the building as fast as he decently could, making for his rendezvous with Hubert.

Jamie moved his creaking body an inch or two to relieve

the exquisite agony and looked at his watch. Ten past midnight. It shouldn't be long now, but he wouldn't be able to sleep peacefully until Fitch and Hubert had done their stuff, and paid the price.

He was lying on the roof of a row of garages facing the doctor's surgery, a perfect vantage point, but lacking somewhat in amenities. He had been there now—he checked carefully—two hours and a quarter. In that time he had seen some fascinating sights—amazing what went on in these classy houses—but no sign of a criminal activity. However, he had been relieved to note the more than casual attention a police car was paying to number 23. For once in his life he was backing the efficiency of the police, and it would be the ultimate irony if they were to let him down.

Now he hoped it wouldn't be too long. Good as the roof was as an observation post, he didn't fancy spending the entire night there. Hubert had the key and a plan showing just where the dispensary was situated. Jamie didn't believe he and Fitch would be able to resist such a golden opportunity, all set up for them by someone they despised and had once humiliated in front of his girl friend. Well, tonight was the time of reckoning. They thought he was simple. Now they were going to find out what sort of a person they were dealing with.

He lay back on the roof and inspected the night sky, which spread itself above him like a rich awning. As usual lately, whenever his mind was free to follow its own pursuits, he fell to thinking about Carol. Tomorrow he would be nice to her, take her to celebrate the success of the Plan. The only drawback was that he wouldn't be able to tell her about it, because she wouldn't approve. In fact, if she found out she would almost certainly never speak to him again.

The thought came like a hard blow, and one which there was no avoiding. For her what he was doing at that very moment was wrong—not silly, or fantastic, or time-wasting, or unrealistic, but utterly and totally wrong.

For himself of course, he didn't see it like that. After all, if he passed up this opportunity someone else would grab it. In this life it was each man for himself. God helps those— he grinned at the aptness of it—God helps those who help themselves. He supposed that was in the Bible. It was certainly true. A dirty fur coat twitched and twisted in a private dance of pain, and Jamie tore his mind away from that subject and back to Carol.

She wouldn't know about this episode, because he wouldn't tell her, and nobody else knew about it. He would collect his takings and then, perhaps, go straight. It was capital you needed for success, and that was what he was in process of earning. Once he'd got it he would see whether honesty really was the best policy.

Car headlights lit up the quiet street, and Jamie sat up to observe. But it was only the patrol car, paying its fifth well-advertised visit of the night, but of villains there was not a sign. He sank back again and closed his eyes, hands behind his head.

When he woke up, it was dawn. The roof was wet with dew, his trousers were soaked through and he ached miserably from head to toe. But these were minor worries compared with the horrified realisation that he had fallen asleep on watch. Had Fitch and Hubert done the job? Had they got arrested? The street was silent, bathed in the gloriously transparent sunlight of the first minutes of a very hot day. He looked anxiously for signs of a felony, but number 23 stood there in solid, bourgeois splendour, its door and windows firmly shut. A milk float purred its way around the corner into the street. London was waking up, and soon it would be too late to extricate himself from what looked to be impending disaster.

As Jamie scrambled down from the roof the full horror of the situation spelt itself out in his mind. If Fitch and Hubert had not done the job, then several hundred pounds-worth of dangerous drugs were missing from the cabinet and he would be the prime suspect, having been the last person on the premises.

Of course, he thought, regaining his nerve after the first shock, the probability was that they had made their call, taken the drugs and left everything else just as they had found it . . . and that it was the stupid, clumsy Metropolitan Police who had bungled things. That wouldn't be too bad, because he would still get his cut from Fitch. The obvious first priority was to find out if the robbery had gone through as planned. He sprinted round the corner to a phone kiosk, found a sixpence and dialled Fitch's number.

It rang several times before it was picked up, but nobody spoke.

"Mr Fitch?"

Still no voice.

"It's Hopkins here. How did everything come off?"

There was a mirthless laugh on the other end of the line, the first indication that there was anybody there at all. Before Jamie could say any more the phone was hung up. He looked unbelievingly at the receiver, the dialling tone croaking away, and pushed another coin into the slot. He tried the number again, and it was answered almost instantly, as though someone was expecting a quick repeat call.

"Look," Jamie said, desperation in his voice, "If you're not going to do anything about it . . . I mean, if you've changed your mind, I want the key back."

Again, only silence on the line by way of reply.

"Fitch, I've got to have it back. Do you hear? Fitch!"

For the second time the phone was hung up and the dialling tone took over. Jamie stood in the kiosk, mouth suddenly dry and cold sweat on his forehead, and pulled the bundle of pill bottles out of his pocket. He looked at it wildly, and then, as though reaching an abrupt decision, he pushed his way out of the kiosk, stuffed the brown paper packet into his coat, and began to run down the street in the general direction of the West End.

With the aid of a passing workmen's bus he reached Fitch's shop inside twenty minutes. It was still very early morning, with hardly anybody about, but already the day was getting warm, the streets slowly airing in the thin, bright sun. Jamie hid his packet behind a dustbin and then hammered on the door of Fitch's shop. There was no reply, which was rather what he had expected, so he picked up a milk bottle and prepared to hurl it through the glass. At that moment he was prepared to wake up the whole of Mayfair if need be in order to get back the key and restore everything to the way it was before he put the Plan into operation.

As he drew back his arm to throw the bottle Fitch peered through the glass and, seeing his intent, hastily opened the door and let him in. Jamie pushed past him into the shop, still carrying the milk, which Fitch removed from his hands and placed carefully on the counter. He was wearing a splendid red and gold dressing gown over his pyjamas, and even at six-thirty in the morning, lighting the inevitable black cigarette, he looked every inch the screen villain. But for once Jamie had no time for dramatic fantasies. The real world, where men usually defeat boys and loser takes all, had closed in on him.

Jamie stood for a moment, fighting to get his breath after his marathon sprint.

"The key, Fitch," he said at last, each word a gasp. "I must have that key."

Fitch looked at him disdainfully.

"You're becoming a nuisance, Hopkins. Phone calls at dawn. Childish tantrums. Disgusting behaviour . . ."

"None of your cat and mousing," Jamie said, hands resting on the counter, fear and hate twisting his face almost unrecognisably. "Just give me that key."

"Now you mention it," Fitch said softly, smiling in a thin-lipped way, "I do seem to recall Hubert mentioning something about finding or being given a key last evening."

"Just give it to me, Fitch."

"Now that would be difficult. Hubert threw it away, I believe."

"Threw it away?" There was no possibility of missing the note of panic in Jamie's voice.

"The key wasn't known to us. It seemed logical."

As Jamie stared at Fitch, the sweat running from his eyebrows down beside his eyes, his head throbbing with the running and now the cold shock of events, the image blurred. Ideas, figures, voices jumbled through his brain, Carol and God and Berman and even a dirty fur coat twitching and jerking in the shadows, and Fitch standing there, hazy, menacing, a superior grin separating the man from the boy, enjoying his triumph.

It was too much. Jamie lunged across the counter, grabbing Fitch's collar and pulling him towards him.

"I'll have it or I'll have you," he snarled, and for a split second had the joy of seeing the grin disappear and fear take its place. Then something hard struck the back of his head and he slid to the ground. Dazed, he looked up to find Hubert standing over him, wearing bright crimson pyjamas, and holding a heavy wooden candle-stick. Jamie licked his lips and tasted blood. He tried to get up, but his head was splitting and he seemed to have lost control of his legs.

Fitch straightened his dressing gown and retrieved his cigarette.

"Chaps like you are two a penny, Hopkins," he said, his voice now openly malicious. "The supply always exceeds the demand. Now get out, will you? You make the place look untidy."

Jamie got up on to all fours.

"Come on," Hubert added, smirking, "you'll be late for school."

He shouldn't have said that, Jamie thought, the miserable little puppet. He summoned every remaining ounce of strength within himself and, under cover of pretending to rise to his feet got himself into position and landed two incredibly satisfying blows. One, to Hubert's stomach, produced a most rewarding groan; the second, to the side of his face, sent him flying across the room and into a pile of hat-boxes. As Jamie made for the door he just glimpsed the havoc he had caused. It was a slight repayment—merely a token, but something—towards the debt he owed them.

Out in the street again, head spinning, blood and sweat all over his face and neck, and on his shirt, he paused to think. He refused to lie down and let them just take him away. There must be a way out, he thought, a way to get the drugs back into the cupboard before Berman discovered their loss.

A sudden realisation was matched by instant action. His mother had a key. He must get back home and lay his hands on it somehow, and then dash over to the surgery before she got there. Although he must have run best part of a mile already that morning, he still managed a sprint into Piccadilly, and an even faster one when he saw the bus coming.

It was ten past seven when he got home. Plenty of time,

he reasoned, so long as he didn't waste any. He opened the front door quietly, clutching the brown paper packet in one hand, and trying hard not to disturb his mother. He paused in the hall for a moment, and then Carol appeared from her room, wearing a house-coat, and obviously having slept very little during the night. It dawned on Jamie that she had realised he was not home and had probably laid awake waiting to hear him come in.

Carol panicked at the sight of his face.

"Jamie, Jamie, where on earth . . . your face!"

"Shut up," he hissed. "Is Mum still asleep?"

"I think so," she said, obediently lowering her voice, following him anxiously, protectively. "Jamie, what's the matter?"

Jamie had already searched the hall-stand, and was now rummaging about on the kitchen sideboard.

"Mum's purse," he said, "Where is it?"

"In her room, I suppose."

He had put the packet down on the table, and to his horror Carol had opened one end and was staring at a bottle uncomprehendingly. On an impulse, playing for everything, he blurted out more truth than she could take in.

"They're from Berman's. I've got to get them back before Mum finds out. For God's sake help me find her key."

Carol picked up the packet, her eyes wide with unbelief. Jamie snatched it from her, and in the process the bundle burst and bottles and packets flew all over the floor. Jamie turned desperately to start recovering them, and found that his mother was standing in the kitchen doorway, half into her dressing gown, hair in curlers, vainly trying to take in the whole bewildering scene.

"What's going on?" she asked blankly. "Jamie? Carol?"

Jamie, down on all fours among the evidence, decided he had come to the end of the line.

"I don't know what got into me, Mum," he said, his voice suddenly juvenile, whining, pleading for another chance. "But it isn't too late. Just give me Berman's key and I'll put it all back before anyone finds out."

Ruby walked over to the table and leant on it, her face

still blank, not because she still did not know, but because she could not understand.

"I don't believe it," she said softly.

"The key, Mum."

"Why, Jamie?" she asked, in a dull, defeated voice. "What ever made you do a thing like that?"

"I thought I could sell them. For money. Mum, just give me the key. Please."

Ruby still stood, unmoving, her face blank, hands on the table.

"I gave you money whenever I could, didn't I? Haven't I always done the best for you?"

"Look, I know you have, Mum," Jamie said, picking up a familiar theme, glad to be back in charted waters. "That's just it. I can't go on depending on you all my life, can I?"

"But, to steal . . ."

"I did it for you," he said quickly, too quickly. "To make things easier."

It was a mistake, and he knew it the moment the words were out. Ruby stood up, and it was as though a great light had suddenly dawned.

"For me?" The words were like a scream of torment. "When did you ever think of me? What do you think would happen to me if the doctor found out what you'd done?"

"He won't find out if you just give me the key. I can get them back and he'll never be any the wiser."

But there was no stopping Ruby now, no putting out of the light, no more tricks to play.

"Don't you realise that job has kept us? It's paid for you at college, put clothes on your back, food into our mouths. For me?" Again the tormented scream. "For me? That's a laugh, that is. You never gave a thought for me. You didn't care whether I kept the job or not. Just where would another job like that come from? Answer me that."

Jamie looked pleadingly at Carol, but she just stood there transfixed, watching this sordid game to its last desperate moves.

"If you'd just stop getting excited," Jamie said, in what he fondly imagined was a pacific tone of voice, "and give me the key, everything would be all right. I don't want to upset the doctor any more than you do, Mum."

At last Carol got into the act.

"Jamie, why don't you go to Dr Berman, tell him what happened, and that you couldn't go through with it . . ."

"You'll do nothing of the kind," Ruby said firmly, "I'll not have him thinking . . ."

She stopped in mid-sentence as Jamie, who had finished picking up the bottles and boxes from the floor, stuffed the lot into her hands.

"Here," he said, "If you're so damn worried about what your precious doctor will think, why don't you take the bloody things back?"

"Couldn't you, Mrs Hopkins?" Carol suggested, very quietly.

"If I do," said Ruby with icy precision, "I'm doing it for myself, not just to get him out of hot water. I've spent my life doing that, and I'm finished."

Jamie stared at her, staggered not so much by her words —she had 'finished with him' hundreds of times before, it was all part of the game—but by the tone of withering reality in which they were uttered.

Ruby deliberately kept her eyes off him, as though she couldn't bear the sight, and addressed herself to the sideboard, speaking quietly, putting into words the light that had dawned, light that was really darkness.

"You accept him as your son, your own flesh and blood. You work for him, give him your life, sit by his bed when he's ill, let him cry on your shoulder when he's hurt. And then he grows up, and you wonder whether it's the same person. You know . . ."—sudddenly she looked at Jamie, speaking to him instead of about him—"I never dared let myself think about what sort of person you are, in case I found that you were just the sort of person who makes me sick."

The last three words were spat out, and Jamie flinched slightly at the undisguised venom she put into them. Nobody moved, and Ruby resumed her soliloquy in the awkward silence.

"Standing there, you're not my son. I'm sure I don't love a person like you. I don't think I even like you. Perhaps I never did." She hugged the parcel of drugs to her chest, like some awful token of doom. "But before I let you ruin me, I'll chuck you altogether. You find out what it's like without anybody to lean on—yes, you, the high and mighty Lord Jamie. You see what I've been to you."

Ruby gestured towards Carol.

"See how you get on with just a slip of a girl to lean on. She's not going to keep picking you up, propping up your big ideas, putting up with your tantrums and your lies and your selfishness. She's going to expect you to keep her." Ruby laughed mirthlessly. "That's a good joke, that is—you can't even keep yourself. You're a great big baby, Jamie Hopkins, running home to mummy when you're in trouble, playing at grown ups. That's all it is—playing at it."

At last the inevitable tears were appearing. Jamie looked to Carol for support, but she just stood there, face set, not lifting a finger to help him.

"Mum . . ." he said, putting out a hand. But she pushed it aside, and walked over to the door, her old slippers making a slapping noise as she went.

As she shut the door she remarked, to nobody in particular, "If I'm going to get there before the doctor, I suppose I'd better catch the bus right away."

It was all happening out there, the traffic roaring by on both sides, the top decks of the buses just visible over the stark walls.

MACKESON—YOU CAN TASTE THE QUALITY
WIN £150,000 for a halfpenny
JOIN THE JET SET
TYPHOO—PUTS THE 'T' IN BRITAIN

It was all happening, on the sides of the buses and in the faces of the crowds and on the news placards: earthquakes, air crashes, love and divorce, scandal and the Third Test, men arguing at the United Nations, other men dying in Vietnam. There was noise and colour and life and death on this sticky June day, the temperature on the Met. office roof being a record for the time of year, shadows long, tempers short.

Carol threw a sandwich to the sparrows and watched the pigeons move in—naked aggression, unprovoked assault—and take the lot. Normally she would have sympathised with the sparrows, but today was different. Suddenly she felt older and wiser in the ways of the world. For the first time she saw what a revolutionary movement she had joined, in following this Jesus—far more radical than all these political agitators, turning the world upside down. Giving, not taking; loving those who hate you; offering to go two miles with the person who compels you to go one. Never before had she seen the human race in quite this light, nor the difference that Jesus Christ made.

And instead of hating Ruby and Jamie for being so crude and hateful and selfish, she found that she warmed to them in their need, not the sparrows but the pigeons; the ones who fight and plunder and struggle and end up full but empty, rich but poor. Certainly she had never loved Jamie more than at this moment, now that he was broken and bruised and helpless, and knew it. All through the morning at work she'd been praying for him, in a way she had never been able to before. She felt for the first time that she might be able to help him.

He'd said he would see her at the church at lunch time, and this was one occasion when she was sure he would turn up. She had no idea what he would say, how he would try to cover up, what excuses he would make. But she knew that nothing could ever erase what happened in the kitchen that morning, and she would never see him in the old light again.

Carol looked at the familiar ruins, and even they seemed changed. It was true that all stood where it had for years, the empty windows, the flag-stoned aisle, and Samuel Sebastian Grey, his works following him, sleeping beneath her feet. The inscription she had found the other day on an old tomb-stone had probably helped in this change. "I am the resurrection and the life", it had declared, and the phrase had stuck in her mind all the afternoon until she was able to ask Gladys where it came from and was tremendously impressed to find that Jesus said it on His way to a graveyard. Life out of death, that's what this place stood for, she had decided, and now it seemed irresistibly true, the walls crumbling, the windows empty, the old churchwarden dead beneath her feet (and the old Jamie dying in the kitchen), and yet everywhere life: the butterflies, the cats, the plants and weeds and nettles and the birds, fighting over the scraps. It was funny, she thought, but the place that used to fill her with foreboding had become a place of hope.

The corrugated iron sprang itself, and she turned to watch Jamie picking his way through the undergrowth, smiling at her and sitting down just behind her, for all the world as if nothing had happened that morning.

"Hallo, Jamie."

"Hi, little bird," he said. "Still feeding those sparrows? One of these days they'll burst."

She looked round at him, her eyes very serious but full of awareness. He sensed her mood and the unspoken question, but couldn't face it head on. He turned slightly, pulling the head off a dandelion and stripping its petals.

"It's not the end of the world, you know," he said.

Carol waited, knowing that there were decent preliminaries yet to be completed.

"It doesn't interfere with my really important plans," Jamie went on. "Do you know, I was talking to a bloke in a pub the other day. He works for the BBC, and he said he'd put me in touch with a recording company who would give me a big break. They're desperate for new talent, that's what he said."

Carol still waited, there being more to come.

"All along only one thing has held me back, and that's good contacts. Well, that and money. You need money for making a demo-disc. But mainly you need talent, and the right contacts. All along that's been my trouble. I wouldn't have got into this last business if it hadn't been that I was so frustrated, knowing I could make the big time but not having the right friends."

He paused, but Carol offered no comment.

"So I think I'll pop in to the BBC this afternoon and see what's up."

Carol knew what she had to say, and the moment seemed to have come.

"Jamie . . ."

But her well rehearsed speech was still born.

"Look," Jamie cut in, knowing exactly what she was about to say. "Perhaps you'd rather I'd lie down and let the next bus run over me?"

She treated him to another wide-eyed look of awareness, embarrassing, but not in the old way. He felt naked.

"You've got to have a bit of hope," he said, very defensively. "If you don't look on the bright side you'll never get anywhere."

"But that's different from pretending, living on impossible dreams." She swivelled round and faced him. "Jamie, do you believe the things you say, or do you just say them . . . I don't know—to bolster your confidence?"

"I wouldn't say them if I didn't believe them, would I?"

"I don't know," she said softly, surprised at her own audacity. "I've often wondered."

Jamie couldn't think of an answer to that, so they sat in silence for a minute or two, several dandelions dying the death, until Carol returned to a direct attack.

"Would it be a shock to you, Jamie, to find you aren't even in the game?"

Stung, he snapped back his reply.

"Any games I don't know, little bird, aren't worth playing."

"Swinging on the outside's no good if it isn't happening inside," she said. "I want my life to be real, Jamie, not make-believe."

"You're living, aren't you?" he said angrily, sensing the line of attack. "That's real enough for anybody."

"No, it's not. Look . . . I've learnt something about myself these past weeks—I'm not clever enough to explain, but I can't be satisfied any longer with . . . illusions."

Jamie turned his head and she saw for the first time what pain and turmoil he was experiencing.

"Carol," he said, as though expressing a deep need and yet afraid that she might not be willing to meet it, "Surely, if you love someone, I mean, whatever they've done, you love them all the way."

Carol looked away, because she had not got used to Jamie like this, letting the covering slip and showing a little of the rather pathetic person underneath.

"Jamie," she said, slowly, working it out, "nothing you do, or have done, could stop me loving you. You know that. I just don't want to make the mistake your mother made, and love a person who isn't really you at all. I don't care what the real you is like, Jamie, I just want to get to know him."

"I've got some catching up to do," he said softly, looking hard at the ground. "But I need time . . ."—a flash of spirit— "and I'm not going to go crawling to you, or Mum, or God, or anybody else."

"You've always been chasing, Jamie." There was no complaint in her voice, just a sad statement of truth. "Trying to catch up. I love you, you know that. But I just can't go on any longer living for the ups and dreading the downs. There's so much more . . ."—she groped for words, beginning to feel that perhaps it was all a waste of time; Jamie was dead, long live Jamie—"Oh, it's part of something you won't even think about . . ."

"Who said I won't?" he objected gently, so gently and so surprisingly that Carol almost missed it.

"Well, you've said it yourself often enough."

Jamie grinned, despite himself, enjoying the look of joy and amazement on her face.

"You don't want to believe everything I say."

"You mean . . . you would think about . . .?"

"Think about it, no promises." He hurried to erect a few safety fences. "I mean, I've managed to get on all right without Him so far, haven't I?"

Carol thought of all the things she could say about that, but didn't. Her head was swimming with the sudden turn of things, that Jamie was even willing to open his mind one millimetre to God.

Eyes still on the ground, Jamie struggled with one of the most difficult, costly things he had ever had to say.

"Carol . . . you know, well, about God and that sort of thing. Supposing—no promises, but there's no harm in knowing—I wanted to . . . talk to Him. How would I go about it? I mean, what do I say?"

Almost afraid to speak, in case some spell were broken by her clumsiness, Carol thought for a moment.

"Jamie, it's just a matter of telling Him . . . asking. He's not bothered how. He can read your thoughts anyway . . ."

"But we haven't been introduced." It was a last touch of the authentic Jamie, and Carol just grinned back at him.

It was all happening now, she thought, the sun beating down and the walls reflecting the heat. Jamie strolled away down where the aisle had once been, over Samuel Sebastian Grey's tombstone, hands in his pockets, head bowed. She could hardly believe it, but she knew enough of God now to appreciate that He didn't do things by halves, and she was happy.

Jamie, on the other hand, was at war with himself. As he walked through the bushes in the bright sunlight he saw other scenes and other places: idols smashed in the sand, people he had trusted and people he had used, Fitch and his mother, and Carol, so different and yet so desirable. And he thought of a dirty fur coat twitching in its private agony of pain in the shadows, and of a flat full of young people who reckoned they knew a man who lived and died (and came alive again?) two thousand years ago. And he felt like a sharp agony the loneliness of it all, the leap in the dark, the little, meaningless acts of self-expression, living and loving and dying, the emptiness of a world where everything happened but nothing was achieved.

Suddenly a few pieces fell into place, not properly or neatly, but near enough to show a pattern.

"God," he muttered, "If You're real, if You're there at all . . . show me."

It exhausted all he knew of himself and of God, and it was barely a mustard seed. He turned and saw Carol, still sitting on her own private rock, watching him. He grinned, and as he walked back towards her the pigeons flew away in a noisy flutter of wings. But two sparrows, small and fat and more trusting than the rest, held their ground and claimed the spoils.

"Come on," he said, taking her hand and helping her to her feet. "It's time we got you back to work."

They walked together out of the church, out of the real world where things were achieved, and back into the world which flowed outside, where everything was happening.